"I foretell that you will love this book"
*Madame Pym, prognosticator, predictionist
and all around mind-reader*

"Simply smashing"
Luigi, lion tamer

"Rooooooar"
Buttercup, the Lion

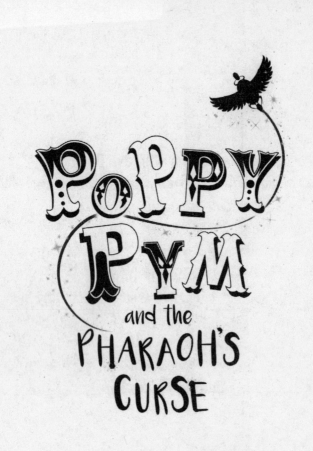

POPPY
PYM
and the
PHARAOH'S
CURSE

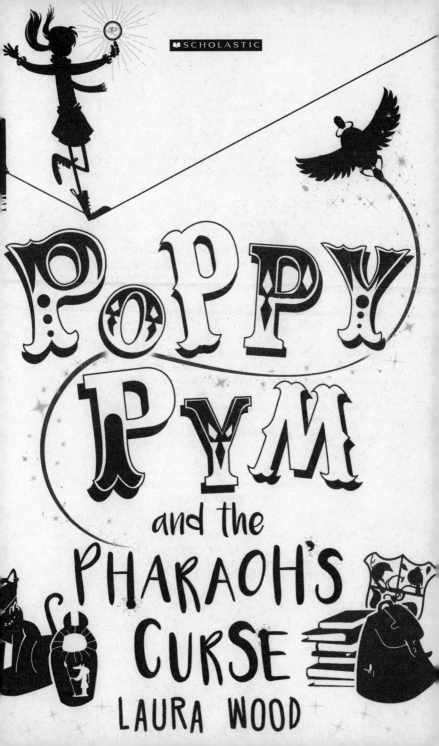

SCHOLASTIC

POPPY PYM

and the PHARAOH'S CURSE

LAURA WOOD

Scholastic Children's Books
An imprint of Scholastic Ltd
Euston House, 24 Eversholt Street
London, NW1 1DB, UK
Registered office: Westfield Road, Southam, Warwickshire, CV47 0RA
SCHOLASTIC and associated logos are trademarks and/or registered trademarks of
Scholastic Inc.

First published in the UK by Scholastic Ltd, 2015

Text copyright © Laura Wood, 2015
Illustration copyright © Beatrice Bencivenni, 2015
The right of Laura Wood and Beatrice Bencivenni to be identified as the author and
illustrator of this work has been asserted by them.

ISBN 978 1407 15854 9

A CIP catalogue record for this book is available from the British Library.

Printed by CPI Group (UK) Ltd, Croydon, CR0 4YY
Papers used by Scholastic Children's Books are made from wood grown in
sustainable forests.

1 3 5 7 9 10 8 6 4 2

www.scholastic.co.uk

To Mum, Dad and Harry,
with all my love.

To Imogen and Alex, who are
funny, clever and kind. I am
lucky to be your Auntie.

And to Paul, who wants you
to know all the good bits
were his idea.

CHAPTER ONE

"What you need, Poppy, is a bit of stability, some *structure*," cried Madame Pym, clapping her hands together, as we hung upside down, forty feet above the ground. She shifted her weight slightly on the trapeze, her frizzy cloud of black hair crackling and sticking out as if she had jammed a wet finger inside a toaster. My own long, mousy pigtails hung straight down like climbing ropes, and I scrunched my mouth into an angry line. I didn't want to talk about this again.

"You need to be spending more time with people your own age. You need to go to a proper school where you can learn about normal things – things it's important for an eleven-year-old to learn about," she carried on. I groaned an enormous groan, a groan that stretched all the way down from the top of my toes to the bottom of my head.

"I do learn normal things," I sulked, and reaching up to scratch my knee, I started to tell her that Chuckles the clown had been lecturing me in the ancient and glorious history of mime and its beautiful melancholy only this morning, when Pym interrupted again.

"Now, you see! I don't think that counts as a history lesson, dear one. You are almost twelve now, and there's only so much we can teach you here at the circus. It's time we got serious about school."

And that was the beginning of this story. I haven't written a real story before, but it seems to me like the beginning is a good place to start. Actually, I suppose I should say it's a bit of a wonky, back-to-front story because in most of the books I've read, children run away from school to join the circus instead of the other way around. I guess you might be thinking that this bit at the circus should be the *end* of my story, not the beginning. Well, stories, like worms, are tricksy things, and you can't always tell the beginning from the end. And anyway, this is *my* story, and if you want a different beginning you can just write your own at the top of the page, I can't do all the work for you. It's no joke being an author, you know.

Now, let's go to the beginning of the beginning and I will tell you about Madame Pym's Spectacular Travelling Circus and the time a beautiful and precious baby was found there. On that fateful night, the circus crew were busy doing one of their late-night rehearsals in the big-top tent after all the crowds had gone home. The Magnificent Marvin, magician extraordinaire, was leaning over his shining black top hat. He pushed his arm deep inside the hat and felt around for a moment, before pulling out a rather grumpy-looking chicken.

"Oh, Marvin, not another one," sighed Marvin's wife – and assistant – Doris. "We'll have to put another wing on the henhouse."

The grumpy chicken shook its ruffled feathers and skulked off, squawking huffily to let everyone know that it didn't much appreciate being pulled out of a magic hat, thank you VERY much.

"Hang on," said Marvin slowly, one arm still inside his hat. "There's something else in here. Something . . . bigger."

"Oh dear," said Doris. "I do hope it's not another turkey; they make such a row."

Marvin leaned over the hat and peered inside. "No, I don't think so. . ." He trailed off as he plunged both arms into the hat, bending down until the top half of his body had disappeared inside it. "Good gracious!" His voice echoed from somewhere far away, and a moment later he emerged with a bundle of blankets in his arms.

"What is it, dear?" asked Doris, peering short-sightedly from behind her thick glasses.

"Well, it's . . . it's . . . COME QUICK, EVERYBODY!" Marvin started shouting, which brought everyone else running. There was Chuckles, the sad clown; BoBo, the happy clown; Tina and Tawna, the horse-riding gymnasts; Luigi Tranzorri, the lion tamer; Sharp-Eye Sheila, the knife thrower; and Boris Von Jurgen, the muscly strongman. Even Fanella, the glamorous Italian fire-eater, came slinking over with Otis, a long orange snake, wrapped around her shoulders like a feather boa. And last of all came Madame Pym herself: ringleader, fortune teller and daring trapeze artist.

"What on earth is the matter?" demanded Pym, who was very tough and very small and had to stretch her neck to look up at Marvin. "What's all the commotion?" she groaned. "Don't say you've pulled another octopus out of there. We had such a job getting the last one back in."

"That was ONE TIME," said Marvin, hotly, but then he remembered the important matter at hand. "Anyway, it's nothing like that," he added nervously, still holding the bundle in his arms.

"Hopefully not another—"

"—chicken," sang Tina and Tawna, who liked to finish each other's—

sentences and who didn't much like all the omelettes they had to eat every time Marvin's hat spilled over with chickens.

Pym looked closer at the bundle in Marvin's arms. Everyone gathered around it in a circle, then gasped when she pulled back the edge of the blanket, revealing the big, blinking eyes of a baby rudely awoken from a very nice nap. A scrap of paper was pinned to the blanket and there was a pause as Pym unpinned the note and read it out.

This is my baby.
I know she will be happy here.
Please look after her.
~E

Then, as if to say "What are you all looking at?" the baby started crying. And kept crying. Very loudly.

Pym lifted the baby out of Marvin's arms and everyone crowded around, trying to talk the loudest.

"What in blue blazes shall we do with it?" cried Luigi, whose real name was Lord Lucas, the fourteenth earl of Burnshire, but who felt that Luigi was a much better name for a lion tamer.

"Poor little mite," muttered Doris. "Here, Marvin, fetch another blanket for the little dear."

"We must call police," drawled Fanella regally, waving a graceful arm in the direction of the twinkling town lights in the distance. "This not our problem."

"Yes! Yes!" exclaimed Tina. "We should—"

"—call the authorities," finished Tawna.

"No," said Pym very fiercely, and everyone – including the baby – fell silent. "You heard what the note said. It is our job to look after her and make her happy. She will be one of us." Pym got one of those spoony looks in her eye that meant she had had A Vision of the Future, and everyone who knows Pym knows there's no arguing with A Vision of the Future.

With that, everyone sprang into action.

"I have a lovely crate that will make a splendid cot," said Luigi. "My own dear Buttercup used to sleep in it when she was but a tiny lion cub." He wiped a small tear from his eye.

"I'll go and warm up some milk," said The Magnificent Marvin, as he disappeared in a flash of light and a puff of smoke.

"But what shall we call her?" asked Sharp-Eye Sheila, fixing the baby with her steely glare.

The baby hid her face in Pym's shoulder but peeked out again to see Sharp-Eye Sheila's steely glare had changed into a very nice smile.

"She is very red. We call her Tomato," said Fanella firmly. "Is beautiful name." And she brushed her hands against each other with two short, sharp smacks, to indicate that the decision was made.

There was a moment of tense silence before Pym broke in. "What a lovely idea, Fanella. . . But perhaps a different red thing would be better, maybe . . . Poppy? A poppy is a very beautiful red flower, you know."

(And yes, if you haven't guessed by now, that baby was me, the same Poppy as is telling you this story.)

Fanella shrugged languidly. "I think Tomato is better name for her, but is up to you."

"Yes, yes, Poppy!" cried the others hastily.

Which is how I became Poppy Tomato Pym.

After some nice warm milk, Pym took me back to her trailer and there I slept next to her bed, in a small lion's crate full of straw.

And that's the story of my first night at the circus, which is where I've lived ever since. Pretty good, eh? I just let Marvin read this first chapter and he thinks I'm a born storyteller, even if he was a bit upset about me mentioning the octopus incident. I told him that it was an important bit of the story and he said, "Yes, important according to Fanella, because she CLAIMS the octopus stole one of her earrings, but that was NEVER proven." And then he got quite cross and his face got quite red, and he started pretending to be a lawyer and saying "I OBJECT" very loudly, so I left him to it.

Anyway, the most important bit of this first

chapter is that it finishes with me finding my way into the circus.* I had a name, and I had a family. I was home.

---

*Marvin would like me to say that another important bit is that you know no octopuses or earrings were harmed in the performing of this trick.

CHAPTER TWO

Now, you might think growing up in a circus is one big party, but let me tell you, it's not all candyfloss and pretty white ponies. I mean, some of it is, but you have to take candyfloss-making class to make sure the candyfloss is the perfect shade of pink and extra cloud-like. And you don't even want to know what comes out the back end of those pretty white ponies. Also, let me tell you something else: if you eat too much candyfloss – four sticks' worth of the stuff, for example – YOU WILL BE SICK. This is not just something grown-ups say, and I have conducted several rigorous investigations just to make sure.

Still, my first eleven years travelling around the country with my new family were pretty spectacular.

I learnt natural history and zoology from Luigi, horse riding and gymnastics (sometimes both together) from Tina and Tawna, and cooking, bookkeeping and astrophysics from Doris (she used to be a rocket scientist and world-renowned inventor). Pym taught me almost everything else, including how to do a Russian roll on a trapeze. But maybe best of all, I spent hours and hours reading with The Magnificent Marvin.

We read everything, but our very favourite books were the Detective Dougie Valentine series. They're about this boy, Dougie, and his dog, Snoops, and how they go around town cracking cases wiiiiiide open, and getting smugglers to confess to their crimes while the police wait outside the door, and Dougie and Snoops are all tied up, hanging over a hole in the floor above some crocodiles, and the rope's just about to break. Brilliant. (And I think right now is a good time to say that this story is about solving a mystery too, but there are no smugglers or crocodiles. (And I don't have a dog either. Even though I would definitely look after one really well and walk it every day.))

One day, just after my eleventh birthday, a big group of children came to the circus. Now, you might think that was nothing unusual, and normally you'd be right, but THIS group of children had a headmistress with them, and that headmistress got talking with Pym and that was why I found myself In the Soup. (That's what Luigi always says when he finds himself in a sticky situation.) The headmistress was from a fancy boarding school called Saint Smithen's and, as I found out later, she asked Pym a lot of questions about me and how I was taught at the circus. Pym told her that I had lessons every day from different members of my circus family, and she showed the headmistress some of my schoolwork, like some of the absolutely ripping adventure stories I had written about ninja squirrels, and my blueprint designs for several new magic tricks. Then, she and the headmistress got their heads together talking about scholarships and gifted student admissions and a whole load of old hooey. Pym went to talk to the rest of my circus family and they all agreed that it was time for me to go to a proper school, and then they ambushed me – I mean, broke the news to me. Let's just say it didn't go down very well. Which is why Pym and I were having an upside-down argument in the big top tent.

"Poppy, I think it is time you went to a real school

and made some friends your own age," said Pym, firmly, over the top of my arguments. "We'll still be here for the holidays. It's not for ever." I felt my eyes start to sting and my bottom lip (or is it your top lip when you're hanging upside down?) got all wobbly in a way that Dougie Valentine, hard-boiled kid detective, would find most shameful. The trouble was, I didn't want to go to school. I didn't want to leave the circus. What kind of a deal was that anyway? I mean, I might have never been to school, but I was pretty sure that I'd rather be hanging upside down on a trapeze than scratching my head in a maths lesson. Unfortunately, crying when you're upside down is even less fun than crying when you're the right way round, so without another word I pulled myself up and nimbled back down the ladder so that my feet were on solid ground and my tears fell down instead of up.

Pym was right behind me, and she put a hand on my shoulder, pulling me round to look at her. She has one good eye that seems to see everything around her, no matter how small, and one bad eye that scrunches up a bit and can see the future. Pym always says that's "one eye for looking out, and one eye for looking in". Just at that moment she was fixing both eyes on me in a way that might best be described as beady.

"Come with me," she said, turning and striding off as fast and purposefully as her short legs allowed.

I scampered after her, trying to keep up with the record-breaking pace she seemed to be setting, and past a large black sign on which in glistening gold letters was written:

You might have been wondering why we all call Pym by her last name, and here is your answer. Pym always says that if you had a first name like Petronella you'd use your last name too, and I have to say I agree with her on that one. Plus, Pym just looks like a Pym. She's the Pymiest person I know, and if you ever meet her I'm sure you'll think just the same. Sometimes I look in the mirror and imagine that my name is Beth or Sarah, but it just doesn't fit – I'm a Poppy through and through. It's just like that with Pym, and that's all there is to it.

We hustled past Pym's performance tent, which was made up of billowing colourful silken scarves and which contained her antique tea set for reading people's tea leaves and her crystal ball. Pym never really uses these things; she says her premonitions just come to her, but that the customers appreciate these little touches. For a while she had a smoke machine and some tinkling crystals as well, but Pym said they just gave her a headache so she chucked them out.

At the back of Pym's tent was the trailer that she and I lived in together whenever we were on the road. This place was a very different story. The performance tent might have been all for show, but this place was home. The small space was crammed full of old, cosy bits of furniture. Almost every available surface was covered in pictures I had drawn or photographs of me and the rest of the circus family on our travels all over the country. I followed Pym into the trailer, where she was already sitting at the small kitchen table. "Here!" she said, slapping something down on top of the soft, flowery tablecloth and pushing it towards me. I picked it up, and saw that it was a glossy brochure with "Saint Smithen's: A Home from Home" stamped across the top in fancy gold writing. On the cover was a group of boys and girls in blue-and-white tartan uniforms, with great big smiles like half-moons. They were sitting on a blanket in the grass in front of an enormous building made of honey-coloured stone. It was beautiful. Here, I'll stick in the front cover so you can see for yourself. I started flicking through, trying not to enjoy the photographs of the cosy dorm rooms, the students toasting marshmallows over a campfire, the giant greenhouse bursting with exotic plants that looked like a corner of the rainforest, and the library. I couldn't help but stop and stare at the picture of the library, with its battered leather

armchairs and walls lined from floor to ceiling with more books than I had ever seen – more books than I even knew existed. *But still,* a voice inside my head said, *school's so boring. Everyone says so. And what about the other children? They'd probably think you were weird. You'd never fit in.*

I looked up over the top of the pages at Pym, and she smiled at me. "You need to go, lovey," she said gently. "It will be good for you. You'll love it there. I know."

"No!" I said loudly. "I don't want to go. I want to stay here with you!"

Pym gave me a long look with her bad eye. "Poppy, love, I know you think it's the end of the world now, but we have to do what is best for you. You need to have a real chance to make some friends your own age and to learn—"

I pushed my chair back and ran out of the trailer before she could finish, almost tumbling over my own legs, as they seemed to be moving so much faster than the rest of my body. I stopped running when I got to a big oak tree that looked particularly sympathetic, and I sat down underneath it with my knees pulled up to my chest and treated myself to a good old cry.

After a couple of minutes I heard a cheerful whistling approaching, and noticed Luigi sauntering over, one hand in his tweed jacket pocket and the other holding a lead, at the end of which an enormous lion was happily trotting along.

"What ho, Poppers!" Luigi called, and he made his way over and sat down next to me, leaning his back against the tree trunk. Buttercup headbutted me affectionately and then sprawled out on the grass beside us.

"Just out for our afternoon perambulations," said Luigi, breaking the silence. "Stretching the old beanpoles and all that."

I stayed quiet. Luigi twirled one neat, curling end of his black moustache. "Thing is, old bean," he broke in, "school, you know, it can be a wonderful place for a gal like you. Meet loads of chums, have some larks, midnight feasts and the like. Even learn a bit, I should think, in a tip-top place like Saint Smithen's. Went there myself, you know, back in the day."

"I didn't know that," I said with a sniff.

"Oh yes," he replied, "back when I was Little Lord Lucas. Had a splendid time."

"But what if they don't like me?" I said quietly. "What if I don't fit in there?"

Luigi looked at me in surprise. "Not like you, Pops? YOU? Place is full of clever kids, isn't it?"

I nodded slowly.

"Well, there you are, then," he said, throwing his hands up. "Stands to reason, dear girl. Only the most terrible idiot could dislike you, and the place is full of clever clogs. THEREFORE, they'll love you. Can't argue with that."

"But won't . . . won't you miss me?" I asked, plucking at a piece of grass.

Buttercup roared mournfully and covered her eyes with one big paw.

Luigi swallowed hard a couple of times. "Miss you? Well, I should think rather frightfully, old girl. Why, place won't be the same without you." Buttercup put a comforting paw on his arm. "Thing is, Poppers," Luigi continued in a slightly wobbly voice, "we're all so terribly fond of you, you know. Have to do what's best for you."

I gave him a watery smile. "But I won't fit in," I tried again. "I'll be . . . different."

Buttercup gave an angry growl and buffled me with her head.

"Well said, my little Buttercup, I quite agree. Who wants to be just the same as everyone else?" asked

Luigi. When I didn't reply, he poked me in the ribs and said, "And if you hate it, then Buttercup and I will bust you out ourselves."

"Promise?" I asked

"Solemnly swear it on the graves of all my ancestors," said Luigi, placing his hand over his heart. "And there are scads and scads of them."

"Well. The library *did* look nice," I said carefully.

"Oh yes," said Luigi. "Millions of books, I should think."

"And midnight feasts *do* sound pretty fun."

Luigi pulled me into a big hug. "That's my girl."

When I went back to the trailer, Pym was just pouring steaming hot chocolate into my favourite mug. That is the nice thing about Pym's visions – she always knows just what you need, and just when you need it.

"I'm scared," I said.

"I know," said Pym, taking my hand.

"But I'll . . . I'll try it." I tried to sound brave, but my voice came out a bit squeaky.

Pym squeezed my hand. "Of course you will," she smiled. "Poppy Pym, you're the bravest girl I know, and this is a big adventure."

And then we both had a big, teary hug. Then everyone else came rushing into the trailer and we had big, teary hugs all around.

"That's enough of that," said Sharp-Eye Sheila with one last sniffle. "Now that it's really decided, we should be celebrating!" She pulled out her trusty banjo and started plucking a merry tune. We all spilled out of the tight trailer, and Tina and Tawna – who had been taught by their parents, who were professional acrobats in China – sprang into an elaborate tumbling routine, spinning and flipping and twirling all over the place. Fanella and Boris began performing an exquisite foxtrot, and BoBo and Chuckles spun me round and round until we were laughing and dizzy. We spent the night singing and dancing and laughing like that underneath the stars, but as I looked around, I felt fear gnawing at me like an anxious rabbit chewing on an equally anxious carrot. How could I leave this all behind?

CHAPTER THREE

The next morning I woke up feeling like a nervous kaleidoscope of butterflies was fluttering away in my stomach. (Did you know that a group of butterflies is called a kaleidoscope? I love it when words make friends like that.) I was worried about making friends of my own. I'd never really had to do that before. I had my family, and we moved around so much that it just wasn't something I had a lot of practice with. None of my books were especially helpful, because as far as I could tell people just *became* friends without any special effort. Why weren't there proper instructions? Were there rules? A special code? A secret handshake? I called a family meeting to discuss this important matter.

My family sat on benches in front of me, and after I raised the question of how to make friends, there was a long, thoughtful pause.

"What would be best," said Doris, "would be for you to get some practice in. Luigi, stand up with Poppy, and then we can see how it goes. Introduce yourself, Poppy."

"But I don't know how!" I said. "That's the problem."

"A handshake is always a good idea," boomed Boris, reaching out and crushing my fingers in his enormous hand and pumping my arm up and down so hard that I found myself being lifted off the ground.

"And you should smile," added Marvin. I plastered on a big beaming smile.

"No, biiiiiiiiiiiig smile, Tomato, like this." Fanella flashed me an enormous grin. I stretched my smile out like an elastic band until my cheeks hurt. "Is good," Fanella said, "but less crazy in the eyeholes, please." I wasn't really sure what I was supposed to do with that particular advice, so I just smiled even harder. Luigi jumped up by my side and I shook hands with him.

"Now, you could talk about the weather, or say something nice," Luigi said, "like this." He paused.

"I say, you're looking lovely today, Pops. Love the outfit." I looked down at my clothes – green leggings with purple leg warmers, a slightly tatty pink tutu and a blue-and-white stripy T-shirt. Nothing out of the ordinary. I shrugged.

"Er, thanks." I said. "I like your . . . face."

"Why, thank you," said Luigi, looking pleased. "I've had it for years."

There was a polite round of applause and Luigi and I both bowed.

"Perfect," said Luigi. "We're definitely friends now." I felt a bit better, but I still wasn't quite sure whether I'd be able to put this stuff into practice.

The next few days passed in a blur. I had to get a uniform, and textbooks, and choose a pencil case, and try out all the pens in the stationery shop. I also carried on with my usual circus chores, and my gymnastics and trapeze training, guessing that even though this school was very fancy, there weren't going to be a lot of opportunities for flying trapeze practice. Somersaulting through the air with a trail of pigtails behind me, I thought about how much I would miss this place. I slept with the Saint Smithen's brochure under my pillow and looked at all the smiling faces inside it, hoping so very, very hard that somewhere in that school I would find some new friends.

In the end, I didn't have very much time to feel sorry for myself. Before I knew it, it was time to pack my suitcase. I was sitting on top of the lid, trying desperately to get it to shut, and just mulling over whether I needed to take eight Dougie Valentine books with me or if seven would be enough when I heard a tap at my door. I opened it and there stood Chuckles and BoBo. When Chuckles, who is tall and thin, is particularly overcome with emotion – like he was at this moment – he can't speak but can only communicate through mime. He drifted into the corner of the room, where he stood weeping. Bobo, who is short and round, has wild curly hair that I help her dye a different colour every week. At that moment it was bright purple, or Purple Pizzazz, as it said on the packet. She burst into the room, fizzing over with questions.

"What are you doing? Packing? What are you packing? Have you packed your umbrella yet? Don't you think umbrella is a funny word? Umbrella, umbrella, umbrella. . ." She pulled some balloons out of her pocket and started creating an inflatable umbrella, and then an inflatable me holding the

27

inflatable umbrella, and then an inflatable BoBo, holding the other hand of the inflatable me, holding the inflatable umbrella. Chuckles's silent weeping became more elaborate and he clutched at his heart before slipping, noiselessly, to the ground.

A large, square head stuck itself around the door. "What's going on in here?" boomed Boris as he squeezed into the room with us. Chuckles began silently beating his hands on the floor.

"Chuckles is a bit upset, and BoBo was just helping me pack," I said. "I can't seem to get my suitcase to close. Might have to leave some of my Dougie Valentine books behind. . ."

Boris looked over at my suitcase and laughed a loud, rumbling laugh. "Oh no, Poppy. I can close that easily. No problems." And he picked me up with one hand and lifted me over his head so that he could squeeze around by the bed. "Pass me a few more of those books. . ."

I handed over an extra six Dougie Valentine books.

Placing one hand on the lid of the suitcase, Boris pushed it closed as easily as if it had been empty. "BoBo, come here and clip it shut, will you?" he asked.

Reaching out to help Boris, BoBo let go of the inflatable, weeping Chuckles she was making and it deflated with a sad sigh. Then she shuffled over, trailing my bed sheet along with her and knocking more things off shelves on her way. It took quite a long time but eventually, everything was packed and then it was time to go.

Saying goodbye is the worst. The actual, stinking worst of the worst. The pits, really.

The whole troupe came out to wave me off as I climbed into Luigi's van with my battered suitcase. Doris had packed me some ham and cheese sandwiches wrapped up in waxy brown paper.

Sharp-Eye Sheila started playing "For She's a Jolly Good Fellow" on the banjo and everyone sang.

The Magnificent Marvin pulled a pound coin out of my nose and handed it to me, before bursting into noisy tears.

Fanella handed him a very elegant lacy handkerchief, which he honked his nose into a couple of times before rolling it into a ball, stuffing it between his fingers and making it disappear. Fanella looked a bit miffed for a moment, until a white dove appeared carrying a large white hanky and dropped

29

it in her hand. She dabbed her own eyes with that as she told me to "Kill them dead, Tomato."

("It's knock them dead, dear," corrected Doris.)

Then everyone hugged me and the next thing I knew Pym and I were tootling down the road, on our way. I waved and waved at everyone as they grew smaller and smaller in the back window, until they were like specks of dust that you could only see if you screwed your eyes together just right. And then I kept on waving for a bit longer just to be sure.

When I finally turned around to face the front, I had a sore neck from where the seat belt had been digging in, and I found Pym concentrating very hard on driving, her seat pressed right up against the steering wheel, and her nose, eyes and hair just poking over the top. She pushed a button on the CD player, and I heard a famous actor with a voice as smooth as a horse, reading one of my favourite Dougie Valentine stories. I was glad that Pym knew I didn't want to speak just then, that I was full to my fingertips of so many feelings there was no room in me for talking. Instead, I settled back and picked at a sandwich as Dougie and Snoops tackled a counterfeiting ring from South America.

Eventually, after we had been driving for a while,

we both relaxed, and it was during a spirited game of I-Spy (especially tricky with Pym, who sometimes plays I-Spy with My Inner Eye) that we pulled up to a huge pair of iron gates and began to crunch over a long gravel driveway. There were lots of cars around, and out of them poured boys and girls of every shape and size. There were children everywhere, shouting, hugging, chasing each other. I felt very small. I looked across at Pym and she was glancing quickly about her, taking everything in like an inquisitive blackbird.

"Well, lovey, here we are," she said quietly, peering over the steering wheel. Then she let out a long, slow whistle. "And very nice it is too."

Pym was right. As I looked through the window, the main school building stretched out in front of us, long and low, with the September sunlight gently warming its golden stones to a rosy glow. On either side of the wide gravel path were perfectly manicured lawns, and in the distance I could see tennis courts and more students sprawling beneath shady oak trees. The murmur of their laughing chatter spilled through my open window. Peeking round the back of the school, I could see the edge of a large, tall glass building full of feathery green fronds and bright splashes of colour that stretched all the way into the impressive domed roof.

Straightening her back, and looking as cool as a cucumber, Pym swerved the van haphazardly into a gap out the front, slammed on the brakes, and jumped out, grabbing her umbrella on the way. I emerged with what I hoped was a totally relaxed smile plastered on my face, but which probably looked more like a mad Halloween mask.

"I don't think it's going to rain, Pym—" I began, but she had marched a little way over to where a couple were standing talking with their daughter.

"Here," said Pym, pushing the button so that the umbrella sprang open in front of the startled family's faces.

"Wh—" the woman began, but at that moment a student came bombing towards them at a speedy pace. He caught his toe and tripped forward, flinging a stream of soda from the open can in his hand right at the umbrella, which it hit with a mighty splash. Pym gave the umbrella a little shake and then closed it. "Th-thanks," the woman stammered.

"No problem," said Pym with a friendly crinkling smile, before making her way back to me.

My knees were shaking as we pushed our way

through the tall oak doors and into a cool, echoing entrance hall. This was also full of parents all shouting things like, "TIMMY! HAVE YOU GOT ENOUGH PAIRS OF PANTS?" and red-faced children trying to pretend they couldn't hear them. Sitting at a small desk in one corner, an oasis of calm in this crazy storm, was a small blonde lady in a very crisp white dress. Pym elbowed her way towards her.

"Hello, and welcome to Saint Smithen's," trilled the lady in a voice that sounded like a particularly frilly bit of music. "I am Miss Susan, the chemistry teacher. Are you neeeeeeeew?" She actually made the word new go on for a long time like that. Pym nudged me and I realized I was gaping at Miss Susan like I'd never seen a human being before.

"Er, yes," I stuttered, my mouth feeling like it was full of sawdust. "I'm P-Poppy P-Pym."

Miss Susan ran a very clean fingernail down a list in front of her. "And exactly how many Ps is that, dear?"

"Four," I gasped, managing to regain a little control over my voice.

"Ah, yes, Poppy Pym, here we are. You're in Goldfinches, room three. Back out the door, round the side to the next building on your left. That's the girls' dormitory. Up the stairs and down the corridor on the right." And she pressed several bits of paper into my hand, including a map of the main building that was so elaborate I thought I'd never, ever be able to find my way around without it. I'm going to put a copy in here so you can see for yourself. Doesn't it look complicated? I always think it's nice to have a good map in a book anyway, it helps you to imagine everything beautifully.

Eventually Pym and I found our way out to the dormitory building and through the labyrinth of hallways to a dark mahogany door with a gleaming bronze sign attached to it. On the sign the word GOLDFINCHES and the number 3 were engraved in elegant script. Taking a deep breath, I pushed the door open, and Pym trotted in after me, towing my suitcase behind her.

We were standing inside a round room with walls painted the colour of butter. Inside the room were three beds covered in thick yellow blankets, and next to the beds were small white nightstands. Two open doors led off at the sides, one into a bathroom and the other into a sort of study area with three small desks and an empty bookcase. My eyes fell on a girl sitting neatly on one of the beds with her

SAINT SMITHEN'S

A guide to your new home

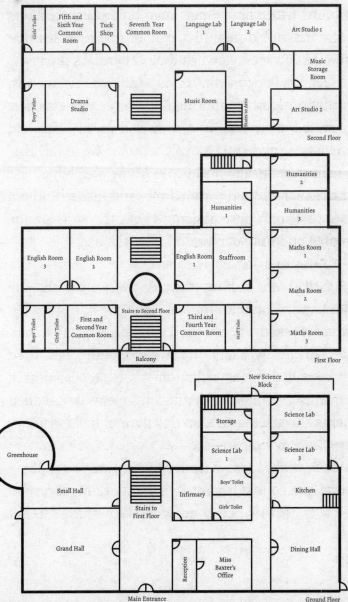

Second Floor

| Girls' Toilet | Fifth and Sixth Year Common Room | Tuck Shop | Seventh Year Common Room | Language Lab 1 | Language Lab 2 | Art Studio 1 |

| Boys' Toilet | Drama Studio | | Music Room | Stairs to Attic | Music Storage Room |
| | | | | | Art Studio 2 |

First Floor

			Humanities 2
	Humanities 1		Humanities 3
English Room 3	English Room 2	English Room 1	Staffroom	Maths Room 1
				Maths Room 2
Stairs to Second Floor			
Boys' Toilet	Girls' Toilet	First and Second Year Common Room	Third and Fourth Year Common Room	Staff Toilet	Maths Room 3
		Balcony	

Ground Floor

New Science Block

	Storage	Science Lab 2
	Science Lab 1	Science Lab 3
Greenhouse		Boys' Toilet	Kitchen
Small Hall	Stairs to First Floor	Infirmary	Girls' Toilet	
Grand Hall		Reception	Miss Baxter's Office	Dining Hall

Main Entrance

hands clasped together in her lap. She was very tall and very thin, with thick sandy hair cut into a bob, a blunt fringe above her huge blue eyes. Her eyes were magnified behind a pair of thick glasses that gave her a vaguely owlish look. There was a pause.

"Hi, I'm Poppy Pym," I said, swallowing nervously, ready to put my friend-making classes into practice. I pinned an enormous clown grin on my face and stuck out my hand. "Lovely weather we're having," I managed. "Really . . . er, you know, weathery." Her eyes slowly drifted towards me, and focused on my face as if only just noticing I was there. Then she smiled and unfolded herself from the bed.

"Are you a Thistle Tweaker?"

Well, I was halfway towards awkwardly shaking her hand when that stopped me in my tracks. "Sorry, what?" I asked, my extended hand hanging unshaken.

"Thistle Tweakers. It's what Goldfinches used to be called in the olden days," she repeated and, obviously seeing the confusion on my face, added helpfully, "All the girls on this floor of the dormitory are Goldfinches, you see—"

"Oh, right," I managed, thinking she was talking complete gobbledygook, "that's interesting."

"It is, isn't it?" She beamed. "Like we have a secret

name. I can lend you my *Bumper Book of British Birds* if you're interested in our house bird."

I smiled back at her but I must have still looked confused.

"Do you know about the four houses that the school is split into?" she asked.

I shook my head.

"Oh, it's just an ancient tradition. Every student is part of a different house – Goldfinches, Robins, Sparrows or Wrens. When you do something good, you get a merit; when you do something bad, you get a demerit; and at the end of the year, they add everyone's merits together, and the house with the most gets a big treat. I heard that last year they actually went to the circus."

"Oh, right, of course they did," I said. "You seem to know a lot about this stuff."

"I read up about it over the summer," said the girl vaguely.

I heard Pym cough from behind me, reminding me she was still there.

"Oh! Sorry!" I said. "This is Pym."

"Oh yes, are you staying here too?" asked the girl, including Pym in her slightly dreamy, beaming smile.

"No," cackled Pym, much amused, "I'm a

long way past my school days now, dear. I'm just dropping Poppy off. And what's your name?"

"Oh no, didn't I say?" The girl smacked her palm against her forehead. "Sometimes I just start saying things in the middle because my mouth can't seem to keep up with my brain, if you know what I mean. I'm Ingrid."

And then we all shook hands like grown-ups. Even me and Pym, because it just felt like the right thing to do. Suddenly Pym got a curious look in her bad eye. Reaching into her pocket, she pulled out a paper clip. "Here you go, lovey," she said, pushing it into Ingrid's hand. "You need to keep this in your pocket at all times. The vision is unclear, but you will need it. It's very important." I winced, thinking that Ingrid would find Pym's talk strange.

"Oh, how lovely, thanks," said Ingrid placidly, as if things like this happened every day. She slipped the paper clip into her back pocket without another word about it.

We all chatted for a bit while I tried to forget that Pym was about to leave, but eventually there was a long pause and she said, "Well, I think it's time for me to push off."

I felt as if my stomach was about to fall out of my

face. Ingrid muttered something about finding the `
library before slipping out the door and leaving Pym
and me to say goodbye in private.

Pym put her hands on my shoulders and looked
at me hard with her good eye and almost as hard
with her bad eye. She seemed to be fizzing with
energy and I knew that she was going to say
something important.

"Poppy . . ." she began, and I readied myself
for some of her prophetic wisdom, ". . . always,
always . . . eat your peas."

I burst out laughing, and Pym did too. She
wrapped me in a big hug, and kissed me on the
forehead. "You are fearless enough to face the trapeze
and clever enough to make magic. You, Poppy Pym,
are amazing. And we all love you very much. Just
remember that," said Pym quietly. I nodded, and we
hugged again.

"Here is our schedule," she said, pressing a sheet
of paper into my hand. "It tells you where we're
performing and where we'll be staying. Don't forget
that we'll speak on the telephone every Tuesday
afternoon, starting tomorrow."

"And write letters?" I asked, my voice a bit
trembly.

"LOTS of letters," nodded Pym, pulling me into another big hug.

And then, suddenly, she was gone and I was all by myself.

Have you ever felt completely, totally alone? Because that's how I felt. Like a castaway on a desert island. My stomach felt sort of hollow and empty, and I could feel tears itching behind my eyelids. I sat on the bed next to the one Ingrid had been sitting on, and looked around at the empty room. Even though it was cosy and welcoming, it felt strange and unreal, like I had accidentally wandered into somebody else's room, somebody else's life. I opened my battered suitcase and stared blankly at the pile of books that sprang out, wishing I could curl up in my own room and lose myself in an adventure, when an older girl with a sheet of shining black hair stuck her head around the door.

"Are you Poppy Pym?" she asked, and I nodded. "Miss Baxter wants to see you in her office," she said, then seeing my blank look, she added, "Miss Baxter, the headmistress."

CHAPTER FOUR

After wrangling with the school map once more, I finally found myself outside Miss Baxter's office. I was bustled in by a very small, very ancient lady with curly grey hair. She was wearing a fluffy pink cardigan covered in crumbs and a lumpy elastic skirt. The room was dominated by a very large desk, precariously stacked with piles and piles of paper. The walls were covered in photographs, drawings and letters. To one side was a tall bank of filing cabinets, and in the other corner was a worn tartan armchair on which a fat orange cat was taking a rather sprawling nap. The cat flickered an eyelid at me, but clearly decided I wasn't worth any further effort.

"Ah, thank you, Gertrude, that will be all for now," said a disembodied voice that seemed to drift towards us from behind the filing cabinets. Clearly Gertrude, the becrumbed lady, was Miss Baxter's assistant. She mumbled something I couldn't quite hear, nodded several times and then left. I stood awkwardly in the middle of the room and noticed two feet in black high-heeled shoes sticking out next to the cabinet from where the voice seemed to have come. Then some legs appeared, attached to the feet, and then the rest of a body, until the whole of Miss Baxter was standing in front of me. She had a round face with freckles across her nose. Her dark hair was pulled back in a messy bun with a pen sticking out of it, and her hands were covered in green ink stains. She didn't look very much like a headmistress to me, at least not the kind of headmistress I'd read about in books.

"Hello," she said, "you must be Poppy. Come here and help me find us a sweet or something." With that, she started pulling open drawers in her desk, peering inside speculatively and then slamming them shut again. I had never seen so many drawers, and the glimpses I caught inside them were mind-boggling. One seemed to be full of glass marbles, another contained only an envelope with a red wax seal, another was full of nothing but pencil shavings, and finally she opened one from which she extracted half a packet of mint humbugs.

"Here." She smiled, pushing them towards me and sitting down behind the desk. "Help yourself. I think this will be a three-humbug kind of conversation. Sorry about the mess. I am usually pretty disorganized, but the first day of term is always especially awful. And I'm trying to help Gertrude, my new assistant, to learn the ropes as well, so I'm afraid things are even madder than usual." She popped a humbug in her mouth and sucked it thoughtfully. "Did you find your room all right?"

"Yes, thank you," I said, sitting across from her and almost choking on my own humbug, trying to sound cool and calm.

"Yes, I have a soft spot for Goldfinches. I was one myself, you see." She picked up a piece of paper off the pile. "About a million years ago, of course." Looking over the piece of paper, she smiled. "Ahhh yes, I remember, you're in with Letty. She's a second year. We often put an older student in with the first years to show them the ropes a bit, although I doubt you'll be seeing too much of her; she's a real hive of activity. And there's another first-year girl. . ."

"Ingrid," I said, wanting to contribute to the conversation. "I just met her."

"Yes, Ingrid Blammel, that's right. Very bright girl. I have a feeling you two will be fast friends." She gave me the kind of knowing look that Pym gets sometimes, and for some reason I felt a lump appear in my throat. I wasn't so sure about that, given that my foolproof friend-making tactics had only succeeded in making me look like a weirdo so far. Miss Baxter smiled at me and reached across to press my hand.

"I know it must be very daunting for you, Poppy, coming to a big school like this. Especially given your . . . unconventional . . . home life, but I think you will be really happy here. I'm sure you'll be an asset to Saint Smithen's with your many talents and quick mind." The way she said it made me sit up a little straighter. "You might find it difficult to adjust here at first. You're a very unusual girl, Poppy." I felt myself deflate a bit, then, seeing my distraught face, she added hastily, "No, no, it's a good thing! I just want to prepare you for the fact that things might be quite different to what you are used to. I'm certain you will find your way; just don't be downhearted if it takes a little time."

I sat in silence, chewing on my bottom lip. Miss Baxter obviously noticed my unhappiness because she changed the subject. "It's an exciting year to be here," she added. "Not only do we have a new science lab, but we will be hosting an exhibition of ancient Egyptian artefacts before they go on display at the British Museum. You'll be doing a lot of work in your history classes in the build-up to that, and I must say there's some really fascinating stuff going into it."

"Where did the artefacts come from?" I asked. "It sounds like the start of a Dougie Valentine book." I had only meant to think it, but the words were out of my mouth before I knew what I was saying.

"Ah," Miss Baxter smiled, "A fellow Dougie Valentine fan, excellent. In fact, a gentleman who was a pupil here a very long time ago left the artefacts to us in his will, under the condition that they be exhibited at the school for a term before going to the museum. He was a real collector and it's the first time some of these pieces have been seen by anyone outside his family for two hundred years. You're quite right, it does sound like the start of one of Dougie's mysteries, although I hope our exhibition will be free from his usual hijinks!"

She laughed, and I joined in – even though a bit of me thought a few hijinks might be quite good fun.

"Anyway," Miss Baxter continued, "I know that this is a big transition, and that things might not be quite . . . what you are used to . . . but I hope that once you settle in, you'll really enjoy life at Saint Smithen's, and if you find yourself struggling do come and see me."

I thanked her and she pressed an extra humbug into my hand. "One more for the road." she said.

On my way out I bumped smack into Gertrude.

"Are you here to see Miss Baxter, dearie?" asked Gertrude, peering at me short-sightedly.

"Errr, no. . ." I said, confused. "I've just been to see her."

"Eh? Speak up, girl. What was that?" said Gertrude, her hand curled around her ear.

"NO, I JUST SAW HER!" I shouted.

"Hmmmph. No need to shout," mumbled Gertrude. "Get on your way, then." She turned her back to me, and jumped when she spotted a tall lamp. "And when did you get here, dearie?" She directed her question at the lampshade. "Are you here to see Miss Baxter . . . speak up!"

Walking slowly back to the girls' dorm and enjoying the feeling of the sun on my face, I heard a loud cry of "RATS!"

I looked around and saw a very small boy kicking the trunk of one of the big oak trees. As I watched, he ran up to the trunk as fast as he could, launching himself at it with all his might and throwing his short arms around it as if he was giving it a hug.

"What on earth are you doing?" I called, before I could help myself.

The boy swung round and scowled at me. "Don't just stand there gawping. Come and give me a hand."

I thought that was pretty rude and I didn't mind telling him so.

"Sorry," said the boy, a little sheepishly. "I was flying my new remote control plane and it got stuck in that branch up there." He pointed up in the tree. "If I was taller, this wouldn't be a problem. Curse my ancestors and their late growth spurts!" He shook his fist at the sky in a dramatic fashion.

"How late were your ancestors' growth spurts?"

I asked.

"Ask my dad, he's still waiting for his," the boy said, mournfully.

"Well, you'd have to be about fifteen feet tall for it to make a bit of difference," I pointed out helpfully. "But I think I could get it if you like."

The boy looked up at me like I was mad. "I hate to break it to you," he said, "but even though you are taller than me, you're still not quite fifteen feet tall just yet."

I went over to the tree, looking up at the branches. I chose a solid-looking, low-hanging branch as a jumping-off point, and in the blink of an eye I had swung my way up from branch to branch, until I was level with where the plane was caught in some leaves. From there it was easy. I untangled the plane and zipped it into the front of my jacket; then I wrapped both my hands around the smooth branch, dropped myself down a little lower and jumped down to the ground, throwing in a neat somersault for good measure.

The boy was standing in front of me and he practically had to pick his jaw up off the ground. Unzipping my jacket, I handed him his plane. He held out his hand, eyes shining. "I'm Kip Kapur," he said, "and can you teach me how to do THAT?!"

"I'm Poppy Pym and—" I began when a familiar voice broke in.

"Young ladyyyy! WHAT do you think you are doing?"

I whipped around and saw Miss Susan, the teacher who had given me the map, standing with her arms folded and a pinched look around her mouth.

"Oh!" I exclaimed, "Well, I . . . this boy . . . I mean, Kip . . . well, his plane was stuck in the tree, so I just sort of got it back for him."

The pinched look didn't go away. "You can't just go arrrround swinging through the trees!" Miss Susan trilled. "You could have fallen and had a terrible accident."

"Oh, no!" I grinned. "Not from that height, that's easy peasy. Fifteen feet? A five-year-old could have done it safely."

"A . . . five-year-old?"

"Well, maybe six." I eyed the tree appraisingly. "Just to be on the safe side."

"And what is your name?" asked Miss Susan in frozen tones.

"Poppy Pym," I said, confused by the anger in

her eyes.

"Well, Miss Pym, you would do well to rrrremember that it is not permissible to clamber up the trees like a monkey at *any* age here at Saint Smithen's. Nor is it permissible to answer back to a teacher when they catch you doing so."

"But, I—" I began.

"That is quite enough!" snapped Miss Susan. "It is the first day of term and so I am being lenient with you, but any more of this nonsense and I'll begin handing out demerits." And with that, she swept off, leaving me standing with my mouth open.

"But what did I do?!" I turned to Kip, completely flummoxed.

"Oh, you just have to look down at your shoes all sorry-like when they get grumpy like that. Just say 'Yes, miss, no, miss, sorry, miss', you know?" Kip shrugged as if being shouted at by a grown-up who saw you somersault perfectly out of a tree was a totally normal situation.

"Well, no, I don't really," I said, with the sinking feeling that learning all the rules at Saint Smithen's was going to be a pretty tall order. "I don't know anything about that sort of thing at all. . ."

CHAPTER FIVE

By the time we got back to the girls' dorm, Kip and I were stuck into a good chat – I told him about growing up in the circus (actually I told him three times before he would believe me, and even then I had to throw in a couple of backflips and juggle seven pine cones) and he told me about his ambitions to be a top basketball player and how he had tried everything he could think of to make himself taller. These attempts included hanging upside down while holding a watermelon, drinking sunflower oil ("because sunflowers are so tall"), and making up his own strange "mystic chants". Needless to say that all his efforts so far had failed miserably, but Kip was no quitter. He wasn't very helpful when it came to learning school rules, though.

"Wow." He shook his head wonderingly, when I asked why you wouldn't be allowed to eat in class, not even if you were really hungry. "It's like you're a space alien or something. Like you're totally from another planet."

"Thanks a lot," I said glumly.

"No, it's cool!" he exclaimed. "It's just that you don't know how any of these things work at all. You don't know what the rules are. It's just . . . kind of . . . strange."

"Well, now I know not to do gymnastics in the trees," I pointed out.

"To be honest, I'm pretty sure that's the first time they've had to mention that rule. It's probably not in the Saint Smithen's handbook." Kip started to laugh loudly, and eventually I joined in. Still, I found myself thinking about what Miss Baxter had said about fitting in, and how Miss Susan had seemed so surprised by something that seemed so normal to me. Perhaps it would be best to keep my circusy-ness hidden away for now? My thoughts were interrupted by Kip, who was explaining how his remote control airplane worked.

We were just discussing the merits of treacle tart versus treacle sponge when we found ourselves standing outside the door of the girls' dorm. Three girls came out of the door arm in arm, and one of them – the one with rippling blonde hair and an upturned nose – muttered something under her breath and pointed at Kip, while the other two giggled. Kip looked around him as if noticing for the first time where we were and turned an impressive shade of beetroot. No stranger to blushing myself, I patted his arm reassuringly, like I do with the skittish show ponies when they're a bit wound up. The girls' giggles grew louder and Kip leapt away from me as if I had prodded him with a big knitting needle.

"Seeyoulaterthen, bye," muttered Kip, as he stared intently at his shoelaces. Before I could reply, he walked slowly back in the direction we came from for a little way, obviously trying to look cool, then, casting a quick look back over his shoulder at the gaggle of girls, he seemed to give up and burst into a full sprint back towards the boys' halls.

Well, what a moonhead, I thought. But I liked him anyway, even if he was a bit odd in the brain box. Still, I thought, here was another chance to try out my friend-making skills. I turned towards the giggling girls and plastered on my biggest grin. "Hello!" I said, sticking out my hand. "How do you do? I like your eyebrows."

The three girls looked at me in silence for a moment; then the blonde one laughed, turned on her heel and walked off without a word. The other two girls quickly followed. What had I done wrong? I stood feeling a bit teary for a moment, then rubbed my nose briskly and straightened my shoulders. With a shrug I heaved the door open and made my way through the cool hallway back to Goldfinches.

Pushing the bedroom door open, I found that Ingrid was back, once again sitting very neatly on her bed. This time she was reading an absolutely enormous and very serious-looking book, holding the pages right up to her thick glasses.

"*The History of the Decline and Fall of the Roman Empire*." I read the title on the front cover aloud. Ingrid jumped, having not noticed much of anything, including me standing right in front of her.

"Fascinating stuff," murmured Ingrid in the sort of cotton-woolly voice you have when you just wake up. "Wouldn't it have been wonderful to be there?"

Her big magnified eyes turned to me, glittering hard like the sequins on Tina and Tawna's most glitzy costumes.

"In Ancient Rome?" I asked. "Yes, brilliant. Lions and gladiators and all that. A bit like the circus, actually. 'Cept you don't get eaten at the circus," I added thoughtfully.

"Oh," sighed Ingrid, all moony-eyed, "the circus. I'd love to go to the circus. I've never been. My parents disapprove of them. And zoos. And playgrounds. And supermarkets."

"Blimey, what *do* they approve of?" I asked.

Ingrid screwed her face up as if she was thinking very hard, and eventually, after a really long pause, her face unscrewed and she smiled. "Stamps," she said. "They approve of stamps. They're philatelists."

"Fi-what-a-whats??" I asked, trying to wrap my mouth around the sounds Ingrid had just made.

"Philatelists. Stamp collectors. They're both nutty for stamps," Ingrid said, as if it was the most normal thing in the world. "They even have an 1840 Penny Black, in their collection." Her voice dropped to a whisper as she hissed urgently, "*Mint condition!*"

"Wow. That's, um . . . exciting," I managed.

"Yes." Ingrid shrugged. "I don't really get it either. I'm a bit of a disappointment to them, missing the killer stamp collecting instinct. It's a cut-throat business."

"I bet," I mumbled, unsure how to respond to the idea of killer stamp collectors.

"What about your mum and dad?" asked Ingrid.

"Oh, I don't have a mum and dad," I said. "I mean, I suppose I do. Somewhere. But I don't exactly know who they are . . . and, well, it's . . . complicated." I stumbled a bit, not quite sure what to say. I'd never had to explain not having a mum and dad before. So I took a deep breath and launched into the whole story – the one I told you, about the blanket, and the note, and Marvin's magic hat, and the grumpy chicken, and Pym and her Visions of the Future. And Ingrid's giant eyes kept getting gianter and gianter behind her glasses, and her mouth had fallen open. At the end of my story she let out a big gasp, as if she'd been holding her breath the whole time, and then she started laughing and laughing, holding her sides and rolling on the bed.

I was a bit worried at first that her brain had

gone a touch loopy because she'd been denying it oxygen or something, but eventually she spluttered, "And you thought stamp collecting was strange?!" And then I was laughing too, and every time we looked at each other we started laughing even harder, and it was that kind of laughing where your face and your stomach hurt so much you think you might actually EXPLODE and DIE from laughing.

"Oh, no, it huuuurts, it huuuuurts!" screeched Ingrid.

"Stop! Stop!" I gasped, holding my stomach to try and keep the laughs inside.

Eventually we both managed to calm down, and Ingrid had just started telling me some stories about Ancient Rome when the door burst open.

A small black girl bounded in, her dark curly hair escaping from under a big, floppy beret. She was wearing a stripy blue T-shirt and had a fake moustache stuck to her top lip.

"BONJOUR, MES AMIS!!!!" she shouted into our faces, and Ingrid and I stared at her blankly. The girl reached back into the hallway and grabbed a smart suitcase, which she flung on to the third bed in the room.

"Off to language club now. I'm France, you see.

I was Spain last year but I didn't fancy dragging that plastic bull around with me all day. Anyway, do stop in if you have time, so lovely to meet you. Byyyyyyyyyyyyyyyeeeeeeee!" She rattled all this off very fast, in one breath, and then with a slam of the door she was gone again.

"I guess that must be Letty," I murmured, turning to Ingrid, and as our eyes met we both fell apart into giggles again.

"Ohhhhh nooooooo! Not again!" moaned Ingrid. "But she had . . . a . . . a . . . moustache."

"Better than a p . . . p . . . plastic bull," I snorted, and we both collapsed against each other, laughing and joking. I don't know if you've ever laughed like that with someone, but there's something about laughing so hard that you almost puke with another person that just sticks your hearts together like superglue. I started to think that maybe I didn't need my friend-making techniques after all.

That night I lay in bed thinking about what a crazy day it had been and how different everything was, and how some things about school so far were better than I had thought, but some other things were just plain mind-boggling. On my bedside table was a photograph of my circus family that Pym had put in a frame for me. I asked her for an extra copy to stick in at the end of this chapter so that you can see it for yourself. I wished they were all there more than I had ever wished for anything. I know girl-detectives-in-training who are nearly twelve need to be really tough, but I don't mind telling you that even tough detectives get a bit sad and scared. I bet even Dougie Valentine sometimes wishes someone would just tuck him into bed or make him a warm cup of milk, instead of constantly chasing him with angry alligators or fearsome badger armies.

I was just starting to feel that terrible queasy homesickness in the pit of my stomach, so I grabbed the picture and looked at it so hard that I could almost feel I was inside it. There was Fanella with snakes wound around her arms; Tina and Tawna were wearing feathered headdresses and standing on the backs of two of the white show ponies, their arms held up in the air. To one side The Magnificent Marvin stood in his spangly robes, with his arm around Doris, who was smiling and pushing her glasses up her nose. Luigi crouched at the front, his arm around Buttercup's neck in a playful headlock. Chuckles and BoBo stood side by side in their full clown suits, and Sharp-Eye Sheila was pointing a knife right at the camera, as if aiming for the middle of the lens. In the centre of the picture, Boris Von Jurgen was holding his super-muscly arms up, and sitting in one ginormous hand was me, grinning a massive watermelon-slice grin. And right there next to me, in Boris's other hand, with one eye screwed up and looking straight at the camera, was Pym. And just for a second, I could have sworn, she winked at me.

I turned off the light.

CHAPTER SIX

The next morning was a jumble of alarm clocks, and lost socks, and hot then cold showers. Dressing in my new school uniform, I caught Ingrid looking at me with a frown. "What's wrong?" I asked.

"Um, it's your shirt," Ingrid said.

"What about it?"

"Well, it's purple. . ."

"Yes," I nodded.

"And tie-dyed."

"Riiiight," I said, thinking we were really stating the obvious here.

"And sprayed with glitter," Ingrid added, sounding suspiciously close to giggles.

"And that's . . . bad?" I asked. "I thought it

brightened it up a bit."

"*I* think it's brilliant," Ingrid grinned, "but *they* won't like it. You have to wear the regulation uniform. It's in the rules. Here, you can borrow some of mine. My mum sent me here with hundreds of them." She tossed a smooth white shirt at me and I quickly changed into it.

I looked at myself in my school uniform – a blue tartan skirt, knee-length white socks, a white shirt and a blue blazer with the school crest on the pocket. Ingrid had to help me tie the dark blue tie around my neck. Looking in the mirror, I hardly recognized the neat, tidy girl looking back at me. I looked like all the other girls. This made me feel a little bit better, like I really did belong, but also a bit sad. Where was Poppy Pym? If I didn't look like me, did that mean I was already changing into someone else? I wasn't so sure I liked that idea. Crinkling up my nose, I loosened my tie a little and pushed one long sock down around my ankle. That was a bit better. I grinned at my reflection, then stuck my thumbs in my ears, waggled my fingers around and stuck out my tongue.

"What are you doing, Poppy?" asked Ingrid from behind me.

"Just making sure it was still me!"

Leaving our room, Ingrid and I stuck to one another like candyfloss to a shoe. There were girls everywhere, shouting and running around, and we joined the crowd of them heading downstairs towards breakfast. One unlucky girl was trying to elbow her way back up the stairs.

"Forgot . . . my . . . tennis . . . racquet," she puffed apologetically.

Ingrid and I joined the queue for breakfast. I looked around at other people's plates, feeling pretty puzzled.

I tapped Ingrid on the shoulder. "Where's all the breakfast food?" I whispered.

Ingrid frowned at me. "What do you mean?" she asked.

"The candy corn? The pretzels? The little doughnuts?" I asked, bewildered. "You know, the normal food?"

Ingrid started to laugh, but stopped when she saw my serious face. "Gosh, Poppy, do you really eat all that stuff for breakfast?"

"Y-yes," I said slowly.

"Right," said Ingrid. "Well, I think that's more of a . . . circus thing. Here we eat stuff like cereal and scrambled eggs on toast."

"Eggs?!" I said. "For BREAKFAST?!"

"Yes," giggled Ingrid.

I shook my head in wonder. Eggs for breakfast – whatever next?

"Just be grateful we're not in the nineteenth century." Ingrid's eyes took on that dreamy look of hers. "Some of their cookery books recommend broiled sheep's kidneys for breakfast."

"Bleugh!" I exclaimed, thinking that maybe the eggs didn't look so bad after all. After queuing up for dollops of the dreaded eggs (which were all right, I suppose, if you like that kind of thing, but wouldn't YOU rather have a bowl of candyfloss with marshmallow sprinkles?), we ate breakfast sitting at long wooden tables in the dining room. The room was grand in a slightly faded and comfortable way. The gold paint on the ceiling was peeling a bit, and the squeaking sound of chairs on the tiled floor echoed around, mingling in with chatter and laughter. I looked around to see if I could find Kip anywhere and noticed him sitting on the end of one of the rows, chatting with a red-haired boy. He caught my eye and smiled, waving at me, and then he said something to the boy with red hair, who

65

turned and gave me a thumbs up.

"What was that about?" whispered Ingrid.

"No idea," I hissed back.

I noticed Miss Susan, the very prim chemistry teacher, sitting at one table eating grapefruit with a shining silver spoon. She was talking to a very tall, thin woman with a bouncing brown ponytail, and a short, elegant woman with curled silver-grey hair and very red lipstick.

Letty was sitting opposite us, with no moustache in sight. Breaking off from chatting very fast and very loud with her friends, she caught my eye and looked over towards the teachers.

"That's Miss Susan, the chemistry teacher," she said. "Don't get on the wrong side of her if you can help it. Then next to her is Miss Reed, the PE teacher, and that's Madame Pascal with the red lipstick; she's the French teacher. They're both quite nice."

"What's wrong with Miss Susan?" I asked, feeling small and frightened again.

"Oh, she's all right, as long as you do as you're told in her classes. Once you're in her bad books, you're stuck there for life. And she hands out lines and detentions like they're sweets." And with that

Letty turned back to her pals and I looked down at my lumpy eggs feeling like I was going to be sick. I had never been anywhere with lines and detentions before. I'd read about them in books, but now their realness swamped me like a too-big jumper.

I straightened my back and pretended I was Dougie Valentine. What would he think about detention? Pah! Dougie Valentine LAUGHS in the face of detention . . . Hahaha! What is detention when compared to man-eating killer sharks? NOTHING. And lines? Dougie Valentine EATS LINES FOR BREAKFAST. Who has time to care about lines when you're busy wrestling with angry orangutans? If I was going to be tough and brave then I was going to have to stop feeling sorry for myself and just get on with finding some adventures. Still, I was happy that Ingrid was there with me. I mean, you don't want to have adventures all on your own, do you? Where's the fun in that?

With a shrill *BRRRRRRRRRRRRRRRRRRRRRRRR-RRRIIIIIIIIIIIIIINNNNG*, the bell rang through the room, and it was as if everyone already knew what to do. I looked around, confused, and then with Ingrid dragging me by the arm, we all lined up neatly in pairs behind the teachers and started filing out of the dining hall and through to the great hall, where all the school assemblies were held. As Ingrid and I took our seats, Miss Baxter came striding out on to the platform at the front, and a hush fell upon the room. She beamed around at all of us, and her wide, freckled face glowed with friendliness. I felt my shoulders relax, and I felt as safe as I did in Luigi's lion enclosure. (Maybe that doesn't sound so safe to you, but when one of your best friends is a lion, trust me, there are not a lot of places that are safer than when you're hanging out with them.)

"Welcome back, everyone!" said Miss Baxter, clapping her hands together. "I am so happy to see all your smiling faces back for another year. And to our new first-year students, an especially large welcome! We are glad to have you here at Saint Smithen's, and we hope that you will enjoy your time at the school as much as those that have gone before you."

I sat up a little straighter as Miss Baxter's eye seemed to catch my own for a moment.

"As many of you know, we have an exciting year ahead of us," she continued, and then went on to talk about the shiny new science block that they had built over the summer, and some different sports competitions and clubs and a load of junk like that. I could feel the air around me starting to crackle with anticipation as everyone waited for the big announcement they knew was coming. Stories about the exhibition seemed to have spread all over the school, and I had heard that it included everything from an army of mummies to Tutankhamen's snotty handkerchief. I was all wrapped up in the cling film of my own thoughts when I heard Miss Baxter say, "Of course, the most exciting news of all is the arrival of the esteemed Van Bothing family's collection of Egyptian artefacts. These will be on display here at the school for six weeks before they transfer to the British Museum."

A hum of chatter burst out at this announcement and, to my surprise, Miss Baxter put two fingers to her mouth and let out a piercing whistle, snapping everyone back into a crisp silence. Miss Baxter was not turning out to be the type of headmistress I had imagined at all. "Thank you," she said, "I agree it is very exciting news. We are very lucky that Sir Percival Van Bothing was a student here – in fact, he once sat in this very room, listening to *his* headmaster – and that he remembered his time here so fondly that he included this temporary donation in his will."

Miss Baxter turned to the side of the stage and I noticed Gertrude, her hunched-up assistant, standing there with a big piece of cardboard. Gertrude's tiny old body was folded into a giant blue cardigan today, and even though it didn't seem as crumb-encrusted as the pink one of yesterday, I did notice holes in both the elbows and a hanky dangling out of one sleeve. Gertrude shuffled over towards the edge of the stage at a pace that would probably have her losing a race to a tortoise with a broken leg. Eventually she reached her destination and with much wheezing handed the cardboard to the headmistress.

"Thank you, Gertrude. Please do sit down and have a rest." said Miss Baxter, looking a little worried as Gertrude tottered back to her chair. Then, hoicking the object on to the stage, Miss Baxter took great enjoyment in spinning it around with a showy flourish. In her hands was a giant poster. In one corner a photograph of a bandaged mummy in a sarcophagus loomed over the words:

THE WORLD-RENOWNED
VAN BOTHING
COLLECTION

On display at Saint Smithen's for a limited time only!

Come and see the famous ruby scarab!
Meet Ankhenamun, disgraced high priest
of Amun-Ra, face-to-face – if you dare!
Artefacts, activities, and more.

And underneath this announcement was a photograph of a gigantic ruby, carved into the shape of a scarab beetle. Even in the photograph it seemed to sparkle and wink at you like a bright star in the darkest night sky – definitely the kind of thing that Dougie Valentine would uncover somewhere. But this was real, *real treasure*. I felt my stomach turning somersaults inside me. My nose was twitching with the smell of adventure, and something in my tingling toes was just telling me that there was a mystery here.

Miss Baxter's face was peeping over the top of the huge poster and she carried on: "The artefacts themselves will be arriving at the end of the week, and in three weeks' time we will be having a grand opening party before we unveil the exhibition. You are all invited, and as a special treat there will be no lessons that day."

A great big cheer exploded from the audience, and I joined in whole heartedly. I may not have had a single lesson yet, but even I knew that a day off and a big party was good news.

"Yes, yes," laughed Miss Baxter, "it's all very exciting. Now, it's time for the first lesson of the year, so run along and be brilliant. Here's to a really wonderful year."

We all burst into a round of applause, and with that everyone stood up and started filing out the main doors and into the sunshine, off to officially start the first day of school.

CHAPTER SEVEN

Luckily, Ingrid and I were in the same class so we headed towards our first lesson together. While we climbed the stairs towards the classrooms, I heard someone calling my name.

"Poppy, OY! Poppy! Hang on!" And there was Kip puffing over to us at full speed.

"Hiya, Kip," I said with a grin, "this is Ingrid." Kip and Ingrid smiled and waved at each other. When the two of them were standing next to each other, Kip's smallness and Ingrid's tallness seemed even more obvious.

"What have you got now?" asked Kip. I glanced down at the timetable screwed up in my hand.

"History, with Professor Tweep," answered Ingrid. She had already memorized her timetable, and it was in her backpack in a neat plastic folder even though she didn't need it any more, instead of twisted up in a grubby ball like mine.

"Oh, cool," said Kip, "me too. Let's all go together."

We pushed through into the corridor, reading room numbers and trying to work out where we were going. Well, Kip and I did; Ingrid may have looked as dreamy as usual, but she seemed to be headed somewhere.

"D'you know where you're going? I don't think I'll ever be able to find my way around this place . . . it's huge!" panted Kip, trying to keep up with Ingrid and her long legs.

"I studied the map," murmured Ingrid.

"What, already?" I asked. "We only got them yesterday, and Kip's right . . . Saint Smithen's is massive!"

Ingrid smiled modestly. "I have a good memory. Once I look at things I usually remember them pretty well. And I'm sure we'll get used to it soon. Oh, here we are." And she stopped outside one of the doors that still stood half open. The three of us pushed through and took seats together in one of the rows of desks arranged in front of the blackboard. Remembering Luigi's advice, I began blasting people hopefully with my biggest smile, but it only hurt my cheeks and seemed to make one boy who was going to sit in the seat next to me back away nervously.

"Why are you pulling that face, Poppy?" asked Ingrid. "Are you feeling sick?"

"Er, no, no, I'm fine," I said quickly and I pulled out my pencil case and notebook.

Now, maybe if you've been going to a big school all your life, you wouldn't understand the feeling of apprehension and excitement swelling inside me like a well-shaken fizzy drink at the start of my very first lesson. Or maybe you feel like that too after the summer holidays, when you've got your shiny new pens and a fresh notebook sitting on your desk, and you're with your pals waiting for school to start. Either way, I was feeling pretty mixed up about my first real school lesson when I spotted the blonde girl who had been laughing at Kip yesterday. I smiled at her, but she gave me a look so chilly it made me want to put my mittens on. Then, slowly and very deliberately, she turned her head away and started talking to the girl sitting next to her. I felt my cheeks warming up like a red-hot whistling kettle.

"Who's that?" I asked Kip quietly, nodding at the girl in a way that I thought was very secret and in the manner of a top spy.

"Who?" asked Kip loudly, swinging his head around and undoing all my stealthy work.

"SSSSSSSSSHHHHH!" I hissed, rolling my eyes at him. "Her," and I nodded again. Kip stared at the girl for a while.

"Dunno," he finally said, with a shrug.

"Brilliant. Thanks for all your help," I muttered, looking over at the girl's back again, hoping that she hadn't seen Kip staring at her.

"That," chimed in Ingrid, her nose wrinkled up like someone had waved some stinky cheese under it, "is Annabelle Forthington-Smythe. I went to primary school with her and she is the WORST."

I looked at Ingrid in surprise, and Ingrid's pale cheeks turned a bit pink. "Well, sorry, but she is. Her dad's some big-shot bajillionaire and she thinks she's so much better than everybody else. She can be really nasty."

I wanted to ask her some more questions about Annabelle, but then Professor Tweep crashed into the room and dropped his books on his desk with a loud thud. Professor Tweep, it has to be said, looked a lot like a bespectacled walrus. (If you look at a picture of a walrus right now, you'll understand exactly what I mean. Go on, it's OK, I'll wait. Are you back? Good. Now imagine that with a pair of glasses, and a little bit of grey hair on top . . . got it? That's Professor Tweep, exactly.)

He also had a slightly grubby napkin stuck in the front of his shirt. So you might want to imagine that too.

"Hello all," he boomed, "I am Professor Tweep. Well, well, good to have some fresh blood around the place. Let's have a look at you. You first years look younger and younger every year." And he peered over the top of his glasses at us. "Hmmm, sorry-looking lot, aren't you? Still, we'll have you bang up to the mark and shipshape in no time."

With that, he heaved himself into his battered-looking chair, which wheezed comfortably underneath him. There was a moment of silence, and Professor Tweep yawned and scratched his ear.

"Who can tell me when the Great Pyramid of Giza was built?" he asked suddenly. Everybody looked down at their desks as if they were the most interesting things in the whole wide world.

"You, the daydreamer," he boomed, snapping his fingers and pointing at Ingrid, who was staring out of the window with a distant look on her face, "do you know the answer?"

Slowly, Ingrid turned her vague stare towards Professor Tweep. "I believe it was 2500 BC," she said in a clear, carrying voice, "originally built for the pharaoh Khufu, also known as Cheops."

I looked at Ingrid like she had grown another head, and then I noticed Kip was doing the same. The thing about Ingrid is that you think because she looks all faraway and dreamy she's not really paying attention, but then she comes out with something like that.

"Humph," said Professor Tweep, eyeing Ingrid over the tops of his glasses, as a Cheshire cat grin grew on his face. "Excellent. Well, well, perhaps there's hope for you lot yet."

With that the professor swung his legs on to his desk and began talking about Ancient Egypt. Then it was like someone had cast a spell over the classroom. Nobody moved, nobody spoke, it seemed like nobody was even breathing. (But, of course, that bit is just what they call poetic license, where I'm using my words to make the story sound more dramatic and interesting, because if we had all really stopped breathing then it would have made the rest of this story a bit difficult, and I certainly wouldn't be the one telling it, what with being completely dead and all.) What I'm really trying to explain is that Professor Tweep was telling us stories that were almost as exciting and adventurous as a Dougie Valentine book. There were explorers, and mummies, and ancient tombs, and lost treasures. Somehow, when Professor Tweep started speaking about these things, he stopped being a bespectacled walrus, and he became a dashing adventurer – his eyes big and gleaming as he leaned forward in his chair, rubbing his hands together.

Suddenly, he stopped talking and pulled the napkin out of the front of his shirt and looked at it in a slightly surprised way. "Hum. Must have left that there since breakfast." He shrugged and dabbed at his face, now hot and red from the effort of such splendid storytelling.

The spell was broken, and everyone looked around, boggling at each other – each of us surprised to find ourselves in the classroom instead of in the hot, sandy desert. Professor Tweep clapped his hands together sharply.

"So," he said, "we will be spending a lot of time with the Egyptians in the next couple of weeks, leading up to our grand exhibition. Exciting stuff, eh?" He swept his eyes from side to side as we all bobbed our heads up and down like those nodding dog toys.

"Yes, you?" Professor Tweep pointed to Kip, whose hand had shot up in the air.

"Excuse me, sir, er, Your Honour, I mean, Mr Professor . . . sir," mumbled Kip in the voice of a boy tying his tongue in the sort of knots a circus contortionist would be proud of.

"Speak up, Lad!" roared the professor.

"Yes, sir, sorry, sir," gulped Kip a bit louder. "I was just wondering. . . Can you tell us a bit more about the artefacts that are coming here – to the school, I mean?"

"Ahh. Yes. Very interesting." The professor stood and moved to the front of his desk, leaning back against it. His hands were clutching the top of the desk on either side of him, so hard that his knuckles were poking up like snowy mountaintops. "These particular artefacts, as you know, belonged to Sir Percival Van Bothing, a former student of Saint Smithen's; a keen collector in his own right, of course, who also inherited a great deal of the pieces that had been in his family for many, many years."

Professor Tweep's grip on the desk loosened as he drifted into storytelling mode once more.

"The Van Bothing collection is truly one of the most outstanding in the world. And not simply because of the quality of the pieces it contains, but because of the story that goes along with them." He eyed us all beadily, and paused, like a brilliant actor, making sure he had our undivided attention, making sure we were sitting right on the very edge of our seats, waiting to hear his next line. He cleared his throat, and then in a hushed tone, he said, "I am speaking, of course, of the Pharaoh's Curse."

CHAPTER EIGHT

A great big gasp blew through the classroom like a gale-force gust of wind. A curse. *A real curse*. Had he just said that? I couldn't believe it.

"But what is the Pharaoh's Curse?" I blurted out, my voice sounding too loud in the quiet, still room. Professor Tweep's eyes locked on to mine with a frown, and I felt my face heating up like a fiery furnace. Slowly, I raised my hand.

"Yes?" snapped the professor.

"But what is the Pharaoh's Curse, sir?" I said meekly.

He smiled a big crocodile smile that showed off all his teeth.

"I shouldn't tell you, really – it's far too horrible and will frighten you all to death," he muttered. "but I suppose that can't be helped. So would you like to hear the tale of the Pharaoh's Curse?"

"YES!" we all shouted, with one giant voice.

". . . please," came a small, polite voice from somewhere near the back.

The professor nodded and returned to his chair. He closed his eyes slightly, a sign that I had already begun to realize meant the start of a story.

"The Van Bothing collection contains many interesting pieces, but the most interesting artefacts of all are connected to the mummy. This particular mummy lies in a beautiful wooden sarcophagus, covered in ancient Egyptian hieroglyphs. From these hieroglyphs we know that this mummy is the body of Ankhenamun, the powerful high priest of the sun god Ra, which meant he was in charge of all the rituals and prayers that had to do with that particular god. Our story begins, so the legend goes, over three thousand years ago, when Ankhenamun was the most trusted advisor to the great pharaoh Amenhotep.

"The pharaoh had many treasures, but his most prized possession was a ruby, as big as a fist, carved into the shape of a scarab beetle. In Ancient Egypt, the scarab, or dung beetle, was an emblem of rebirth – the way it rolled its dung ball along the ground was similar to the way they thought the sun god Ra rolled across the sky each day. The pharaoh believed that his precious scarab beetle was somehow the key to his own regeneration and so he guarded it jealously. The story goes that the ruby was bewitched: that it was so beautiful, so tempting, that it would dazzle anyone who looked at it for too long to the point of madness. The desire to own the ruby drove several men insane, as their obsession consumed them, and in fact, a few unsuccessful efforts were even made to steal the scarab from the locked chamber in which the pharaoh kept it safely hidden. Those who were caught were buried alive, their tormented souls destined to haunt the ruby for all eternity."

I could already feel my heart hammering like a tap-dancing gerbil. My detective senses were tingling, and I pulled out my notebook, furiously scribbling down Professor Tweep's every word.

"One day Ankhenamun came to the pharaoh with a prophecy," the professor continued. "Ankhenamun told the pharaoh that the ruby scarab would be stolen in the next three days, and that the pharaoh himself would not live for more than twenty-four hours after the theft took place. The pharaoh was frightened, and he immediately went to the special chamber where his ruby was kept. There it was, safe and sound, sparkling wonderfully. The pharaoh picked it up and vowed that for the next three days it would not leave his side. He kept the ruby with him wherever he went, and when he slept, he slept with the scarab under his pillow, and with fifty guards posted outside his bedroom doors. On the third morning he awoke to find the ruby scarab had disappeared. The pharaoh shouted, and in rushed the fifty guards, all of them swearing that no one had entered or exited the room all night. They tore the bedroom apart, searching for the ruby, until eventually one of the soldiers gave a cry. In the corner of the room, under one of the stones on the floor, they found a tunnel, one that must have taken many months to dig, and that led out past the edge of the palace. Whoever had crept in and stolen the ruby had escaped that way hours earlier.

"The pharaoh was furious, and terrified, knowing that according to the prophecy he did not have long left to live. He had the tunnel blocked up and locked himself in his room, this time with one hundred guards stationed outside. He had all his food and drink brought to him by a trusted servant who had to taste everything before the pharaoh would have any himself, and who had to sit at the pharaoh's side while he slept. The pharaoh summoned Ankhenamun to his room and told him that he had placed a curse on the ruby scarab, that whoever had stolen it would come to an untimely end, and that the spirit of the pharaoh himself would haunt whoever possessed it. Ankhenamun tried to soothe the pharaoh, but he was in a towering rage and he shouted terrible curses, vowing revenge on the thief in this life and the next."

A collective shudder ran around the room, and Professor Tweep's voice dropped down lower.

"The next morning the guards opened the door and found both the servant and the pharaoh were dead, an empty wine glass still gripped in the pharaoh's cold hand. He had been poisoned. The ruby scarab was not found, and the kingdom was dealt another blow when, only two days after the death of the pharaoh, his beloved advisor Ankhenamun dropped down dead as a stone.

"Two hundred years ago, when Ankhenamun's

tomb was discovered by Sir Percival Van Bothing's ancestor, Lord Anthony Van Bothing, archaeologists carefully examined the mummies' remains, and when they unwrapped the bandages, imagine their shock when they found, in the space where the priest's heart had once been, the precious ruby scarab beetle sparkling there instead. It had been Ankhenamun himself who had stolen it, and who on his deathbed had ordered his servants to conceal it inside his mummified body so that he could keep it all to himself even after death. He was very cunning, you see – by bringing his so-called prophecy to the pharaoh, Ankhenamun had tricked him into removing the ruby from the safe chamber in which it was usually hidden. He must have been planning for months, digging his tunnel, all the time consumed by his own obsession. I leave it up to you to decide whether his death was simply a coincidence or whether the Pharaoh's Curse had claimed its first victim!"

Professor Tweep finished his story with a flourish of his hand and a stroke of his moustache, clearly enjoying the look on our gobsmacked faces. After a small pause, everyone started talking at once.

"But what happened next?"

"Is the curse real?"

"Did anyone else get hurt?"

"Is that the ruby beetle that was on the poster this morning?"

The questions wriggled all over one another like a basket full of puppies, each person trying to make their voice the loudest.

"That's enough!" shouted Professor Tweep, and the whole room fell silent again. "Yes, the ruby beetle is the same one that was on the poster. Both the scarab and the mummy of Ankhenamun will be appearing in the exhibition, so you may see them for yourself" – he paused dramatically – "if you dare!"

"But what about the curse?!" squeaked the girl sitting next to Annabelle Forthington-Smythe.

"Ah, yes, the curse. . ." sighed the professor. "Yes, it is interesting indeed. There are those who claim that the curse exists. And it is true that the Van Bothing family have had more than their fair share of bad luck since they discovered the ruby."

"What do you mean, professor?" asked Annabelle in a wispy, lisping little voice. "The Van Bothing family were *very* rich and successful. Sir Percy was a *great* friend of my father." She smiled around the room, smugly, her blue eyes like two little ice chips.

"Ahhh, yes, but at what cost, eh?" asked Professor Tweep, rubbing his balding head. "There were so many tragedies in that family," he muttered, picking up his napkin once more to rub his red face as he stared into the distance "They've had such terrible luck for a long time now." His musing was interrupted by the shrill twang of the school bell, and this seemed to snap the professor out of his daydream. "Yes, well, superstitious nonsense, of course. That's quite enough of that. Humph. Now, off you go to your next lesson. No dilly-dallying!"

CHAPTER NINE

The rest of the day was a bit of a blur. All anyone could talk about was the curse, and the story that Professor Tweep told us was unravelling like a badly knitted jumper as it got passed from person to person. At one point I heard two boys talking about it, and one of them said, "I heard the mummy comes back to life every Thursday and eats brains and mashed potatoes."

Then the other replied very seriously, "I heard it was eyeballs and custard."

Ingrid, Kip and I decided to eat our lunch sitting under a tree outside, and we lay on our stomachs, munching apples and swapping theories on how the curse worked, when Ingrid raised a point that made me feel like someone had slipped ice cubes down the back of my shirt.

"You know," she said dreamily, "what's really interesting to consider is that if the curse is real, then who's being cursed now?"

"What d'you mean?" asked Kip, propping himself up on one elbow.

"Well, if it's the owner of the ruby that's cursed, doesn't that mean that when it arrives tomorrow the school will be cursed?" Ingrid turned the blast of her eyes on both of us like a pair of bright, shining headlights.

The air shivered and the three of us looked first at one another, and then all around, as if we expected the school to just give up and fall down out of fright. As I looked at the solid, reassuring building in front of us, the thought of the curse started to seem so silly that I began to laugh. Ingrid and Kip joined in, and pretty soon our conversation had turned to different things.

Somehow, though, I couldn't shake the idea of the curse for the rest of the day. It peeked around the corners of my brain at the most inconvenient times, like when Madame Pascal was asking me to conjugate a French verb, or when Kip was trying to get my opinion on his latest plan to get taller ("I'm thinking if you and Ingrid tie my arms and legs to two bicycles and ride really hard in opposite directions. . .").

According to the schedule Pym had pressed into my hands the day before, that evening was our first chance to speak on the telephone. So at six o'clock precisely, I headed for the library.

The library was even more beautiful than it had looked in the brochure for Saint Smithen's. The floors were made of a dark, polished wood, the walls crowded with bookcases overflowing with books. The ceiling was high and airy, painted with a mural of a cloudy sky. Comfy, creaking armchairs were hidden in cosy nooks, just begging for you to sink into them with a good book in your hands.

I walked over to the wall of old-fashioned payphones in one corner. There were a few students already using them, so I had to wait my turn. I looked anxiously at my watch. A girl with her back to me was talking very loudly.

"Yes, Mum," she said, "of course I'm brushing my teeth. . . Yes, Mum. . . Yes, Mum. . . No, I didn't know that chewing gum makes all your teeth fall out." The girl turned to face me and rolled her eyes.

"OK, Mum. Got it. Byyyye." With a flourish she hung up the phone. "Parents!" she said to me with another eye roll as she brushed past.

"Um . . . yeah," I replied weakly.

I carefully dialed the long string of numbers Pym had written down. The phone rang for some time before a croaky voice answered.

"'Ello? The Flying Ferret, haunted hotel to the stars," wheezed the voice.

"Hi, Leaky Sue!" I exclaimed.

"Poppy! 'Ow are you, my love?" came the reply.

"I'm OK, thanks," I said. "Is Pym there?"

Leaky Sue cackled loudly. "Oh, there's an 'ole lot of 'em here waiting to talk to you, my girl. Wait a second, I'll go and fetch 'em."

There was a crackling sound and a long pause. The Flying Ferret is one of our very favourite places to stay. We always stop there when we have a performance close by. They do the best fish-finger sandwiches in the whole world. It isn't really haunted, but Leaky Sue says that a ghost or two is good for business.

"Poppy?" Pym's voice rushed down the phone line and my eyes filled up with tears as I realized just how much I missed her.

Hang on. When there are phone conversations in a Dougie Valentine book they are all typed out like a script. I really like that because then you and your friends can read them out in all the different voices. Me and Marvin always have a great time doing that. I'm going to write our phone call out like that now so you can have a go at reading it out loud. (Unless you're on the train. Probably best not to do it then. Otherwise people might think you are a bit mad.)

Beginning of transcript

Pym: Poppy?

Me: Pym!

Pym: Are you having a good time? Settling in OK?

Me: . . . Mostly. I think so. Some of the rules are a bit strange and it's all a bit . . . big . . . but . . . there's a real-life mystery here!

Pym: What sort of mystery?

Me: Professor Tweep, my history teacher, told us about a curse on an ancient Egyptian ruby beetle. It's part of the exhibition that's coming here!

Pym: Ooooh. Spooky. Is that the Ankhenamun exhibition?

Me: Yes, how did you know that?

Pym: I was reading something about that this morning. Hang on, let me go and have a look for it. There are some other people waiting to talk to you. . .

Brief pause. Scuffling noises. Muffled shouting

Fanella: TOMATO, IS YOU?

Me: Yes, Fanella, it's me . . . but I can hear you fine, you don't need to shout.

Fanella: I NO SHOUT, TOMATO. IS THIS TERRIBLE LUIGI BREATHING IN MY EAR AND I CAN NO HEAR MYSELF THINK.

Luigi: (*muffled and indignant*) I say, that's a bit rich after you bit my arm to get to the phone first.

Fanella: IGNORE HIM, TOMATO. HE IS CONFUSED AND LITTLE BIT MAD. AHHH. WE MISS YOU, MY LITTLE ONE. IS NOT THE SAME WITHOUT YOU. I—

Luigi: (*in the background*) Stop hogging

the phone, Fanella. Can't you see Buttercup is getting restless?

Distant roar. More scuffling noises

Luigi: (*slightly breathless*) What ho, Poppers!

Me: Er, did you say Buttercup was there? Does Leaky Sue know you've brought a lion inside?

Luigi: (*slight, guilty pause*) Well, ahem . . . well. She doesn't exactly know, but I snuck her in to talk to you. Poor little thing has been so sad since you left I knew she would want to hear your voice. Hang on. . .

Me: Wait, what?! Luigi? Are you there?

Luigi: I'm just propping the phone up so she can hear you.

Me: Oh right. Um . . . hello, Buttercup?

Buttercup: Rooooooooooar!

Loud crunching sounds

Luigi: (*muffled*) Ahhh, she's chewing on the phone. She must miss you terribly.

A scream in the background

Woman's voice: Oh my goodness! Is that . . . a . . . a . . . lion?!

Fanella: IS GHOST LION. WOOOOOOOO.

Luigi: Ahem, yes, ghost lion. Wooooooo. Haunted hotel, what.

Buttercup: Roooooooar!

Luigi: Blast, she's fainted.

Clunking noises, sound of footsteps

Leaky Sue: 'Ere, Luigi! You'd better not have snuck that bloomin' lion in again! I've told yer already that lions is a step too far for the guests.

Luigi: Ahem. Sorry, what lion?

Leaky Sue: Do yer think I can't see you've got a blinkin' lion there dressed up in a scarf and hat? Get 'er outside in 'er trailer. NOW.

Scuffling noise as phone is picked up again

Fanella: HELLO, TOMATO? ARE YOU STILL THERE?

Me: Yes, Fanella, I'm still here. (*whispering*) But the boy on the phone next to me looks a bit scared. I think he can hear Buttercup roaring. Is everything OK?

Fanella: ALL IS NOW FINE. THE SILLY LUIGI HAS TAKEN HIS CAT OUTSIDE. I TELL HIM HE SHOULD HAVE PUT GLASSES AND PRETEND MOOOSTACHE ON HER AS WELL BUT HE NEVER LISTEN. WAIT . . . HERE IS PYM BACK. GOODBYE, TOMATO!

Rustling sound

Pym: Right, I found that article in *Brilliant Beasts and Crazy Curses* that I was reading this morning, and I was right. It's got a lot to say about your Ankhenamun. Nasty business.

Me: Oh, wow. Can you send it to me?

Pym: Of course I can — I'll pop it in with my letter. Did you have a nice chat with Luigi and Fanella? The others are out rehearsing but they all send their love.

Me: Um, yes, it was . . . lovely.

Long pause, scuffling

Me: Hello?

Pym: (*big sigh*) Sorry, Poppy. Luigi and Fanella seem to be trying to cover Buttercup in an old sheet. I wonder what on earth is going on?

Fanella: (*in background*) NOW MAKE THE EYE HOLES.

Me: I think they might be trying to make a ghost lion.

Pym: Oh, of course. I'd better go and sort them out, poppet.

Buttercup: Roarrrr!

End of transcript

I smiled and hung up the phone, but then I felt such

an enormous wave of homesickness rush up inside me that it sort of burst out of me in floods of tears. I wondered if coming to Saint Smithen's was a big mistake. Wouldn't I be better off tucked up in bed at Leaky Sue's with my family, where I belonged? I tried to shake myself out of it, and wiped my snotty nose on my sleeve. Luckily the library was deserted now, except for Mr Fipps, the librarian, who was snoring at his desk and so nobody had seen me cry like a big baby.

I shuddered as I realized how dark and spooky it was in here. I wondered what the article Pym had found would say about the curse. I felt the same as I did in that whooshing moment on the trapeze just before you step off the platform. The ruby scarab would soon be arriving. What new adventures was it bringing with it? And did they spell trouble for us at Saint Smithen's?

CHAPTER TEN

You know those days where everything just goes completely wrong? I mean, really, EVERYTHING. When you can't seem to do anything right? Well, that was my second day at Saint Smithen's.

It started with a broken alarm clock, and Ingrid tugging at my arm.

"Poppy! Poppy! Get up! We are going to be late!"

Ingrid, Letty and I scrambled around the room, bashing into one another while we tried to get ready in super-speedy time.

"Where is my maths textbook?" muttered Ingrid, burrowing through one of the drawers and flinging clothes everywhere so that it was raining blue-and-white tartan.

"Did you look under the bed?" I asked as a pair of socks hit me in the face.

Ingrid dived under the bed, her feet waving around in the air. "Oh yes, got it!" she cried, wriggling out and stuffing the book into her already bulging backpack.

"What clubs have I got today?" asked Letty, wide-eyed and panicky. She looked at the elaborate wall chart she had drawn up next to her bed. "Hockey, photography, debate and pottery. Phew! Thank goodness it's a light day," she said, trying to button her shirt over her pyjamas.

Eventually we all bustled out of the door, round to the main building, and screeched down the corridor to the dining hall.

"Where've you been?" asked Kip.

"Alarm didn't go off," I said, rubbing my eyes.

"All right, see you later." Kip shrugged on a backpack almost as big as he was and left. We were still shovelling bowls of the last squashed and sad-looking cornflakes into our faces (cornflakes! For breakfast!) when the bell rang.

"Not a very good start to the day," said Ingrid mildly. Somehow she seemed to have shrugged off this morning's madness already. She looked like her neat, dreamy self, and as she drifted off towards our first lesson I huffed along after her.

On our way up the stairs we got stopped by a big girl whose gingery hair was pulled back in a tight bun. On her jacket shone a large badge with PREFECT on it.

"Whoa there, shrimps," she called as we scuttled past. "Where are you going in such a hurry?"

"We're late for maths!" I said desperately.

"And your shirt is untucked," she said, looking at me critically. "You can get a demerit for that, you know."

I felt my face warming up, and I carefully tucked my shirt in. "Sorry," I mumbled.

"Recite the school song, please," the girl snapped.

"W-what?" I stammered.

"Any prefect can stop a student and ask them to recite the school song. It's in the rules," the girl said.

The rules again. I cursed the rules loudly in my head. Who'd ever heard of so many rules?! What was the school song? I desperately racked my brain but my mind was absolutely blank.

Ingrid's voice rang out loud and clear.

"Brave and wise and true are we,
Standing proud for all to see,
Goldfinches, Sparrows,
Robins and Wrens,
Though the road may narrow
Our courage ne'er bends
We are Saint Smithen's through and through
The best of brave and wise and true."

The girl nodded briskly and turned to look at me. There was a painful pause.

"Er, we are the birds," I warbled tunelessly. "And we, er, walk down the road. . . Um, Saint Smithen's. Yeeeeeah." I finished with a weak fist pump and what I hoped was a winning grin. There was another pause.

"You'd better see that your friend learns it," the girl said, jerking her head at me. "Now, off to lessons, shrimps. You really are late now." With a toss of her head, she stalked down the stairs.

"What a beast!" I said, indignantly. "We're really late now because SHE made us late. And why did she keep calling us shrimps?"

"That's what they call the first years," Ingrid shrugged.

"And how did you know the words to that song?" I asked, throwing my hands in the air. "I'd never even heard of it."

"It's all in the handbook," said Ingrid. "Didn't you read it?"

"What that great big, enormous, hulking thing they gave us YESTERDAY?" I exclaimed. "No, I didn't manage to get through it all yet. You're so clever, Ing. How'd you read all of that so quickly?"

"I'm just a fast reader is all," she said. "Anyway, I don't think much to the song, do you? I mean, wrens and bends? Not a perfect rhyme. Written in 1848, I believe, by the Honourable Hugo Ferryweather. Fancied himself a bit of a poet. Wore a lot of lacy collars. Became a banker in the end."

I shook my head with a smile. There was a lot going on in Ingrid's brain, and I liked occasionally getting a peek into that mad world of hers.

Eventually we bustled into Dr MacDougal's maths class. Dr MacDougal is quite small and as round as one of Tina and Tawna's hula hoops. Her small, round eyes were looking at us from underneath two rather beetley eyebrows drawn together in a frown.

"And who do we have here?" Dr MacDougal asked softly.

"Ingrid Blammel, miss," said Ingrid, her eyes looking at her shoes, and her hands clasped in front of her.

I quickly copied Ingrid's pose. "Poppy Pym, miss," I said.

"Well, Ingrid Blammel and Poppy Pym," the soft rumble of her voice continued, "in MY class we arrive on time. Don't let it happen again or there will be consequences. Take your seats, please, and we'll continue."

My face as red as my namesake, I shuffled into a seat and pulled out my maths textbook. The problem was that the classroom was so warm, and Dr MacDougal's voice was so droning, and maths was so horribly boring, that pretty soon my attention melted away from the classroom. I was deep in an imaginary mystery, solving crime alongside my best friend, Dougie Valentine, when suddenly I heard my name.

I looked up with a jump to find Dr MacDougal standing in front of me.

"MISS PYM," she said crossly. "Am I boring you?"

"Yes, miss," I said quickly and then blushed as a

burst of stifled giggling swept around the classroom. "I mean, no, miss. Sorry, miss."

"And what is the answer to the problem on the blackboard?" Dr MacDougal asked.

I looked hopelessly at the long string of numbers and letters that appeared on the board and down at my notebook. It was blank except for a doodle of a clown in the margin. "I-I-I don't know," I stuttered.

"Well then," said Dr MacDougal drily, "perhaps you had better pay closer attention, Miss Pym. Especially after arriving late." She marched over to her desk and made a note. "And I'm afraid that's a demerit for you."

I sat for the rest of the lesson feeling terrible. A demerit! On the second day of school! How was I ever going to do well if I couldn't get the hang of things? *Perhaps they'll expel me*. The thought made me go all icy cold and my skin prickled. To be sent home in disgrace – I couldn't bear it.

That evening I met up with Ingrid and Kip in the common room for first and second years, and they tried to cheer me up.

"It's just a demerit, Poppy," said Kip with a yawn. "Trust me, people get them alllll the time. I heard that one year some of the kids had a contest to see who could get the most in a week. It's really no big deal."

"It is to me," I said quietly. "I'd never even heard of demerits until two days ago and now I've already got one because I haven't got a clue what I'm doing. You and Ingrid haven't got one."

Kip stood up and untucked his shirt. "Well, come on, then," he said, "if that's what's bothering you, let's roam the halls in search of a demerit!"

Ingrid jumped up too. "Yes, and if anyone asks me to say the words to the Saint Smithen's song, I'll tell them I've never heard of it."

I was already laughing. "OK, OK," I said, "I get it, I'm worrying too much. Don't go looking for demerits on my behalf." I think Kip actually looked a bit disappointed.

"Anyway," said Ingrid very casually, looking at me out the corner of her eye, "the stuff for the exhibition arrives tomorrow . . . and you know what that means. . ."

"I know what you're doing, Ingrid Blammel," I said, smiling, "trying to distract me! And it's worked! Go on, then, what does it mean?"

"It means the CUUUUUUUURSE, OF COURSE!!"

yelled Kip dramatically. "Wooooooooooo!"

But later that night, as Ingrid and I were walking back to Goldfinches in the dark and quiet, I couldn't help wondering with a shiver what would happen when the ruby arrived.

CHAPTER ELEVEN

Luckily for me, Thursday was a lot better than Wednesday had been. For one thing, I had my first-ever art class. When we shuffled into the classroom, we found that the big, wide windows had been covered with a dark, gauzy material and the room was filled with an almost blue light. Different-coloured paint was smeared everywhere, and colourful lanterns hung from the ceiling, sending strange shadows dancing across the walls. There were easels holding blank canvases arranged in a circle around the room, and in the middle stood a man with a white beard. He was staring thoughtfully at something that I couldn't quite see and he didn't seem to notice us all standing there. Somebody cleared their throat awkwardly and the man spun around, his eyes shining.

"Isn't it moving? Transcendent?" he whispered, moving to one side to allow us a better look at the object. We shuffled closer, and I stared in astonishment at what seemed to be a tower of toilet rolls with wire coat hangers sticking out of it.

"Um, what *is* it?" ventured Kip at last.

The man spun around and fixed Kip with his twinkling stare. "Ahhh, what indeed?" he said happily. "The wondrous curiosity of youth. What do you see, child?"

Kip didn't look very pleased at being called child like that and he wrinkled his nose in the direction of the object in question. "Well, I don't really think it looks like anything," he said finally in an apologetic voice.

"EXACTLY!" cried the man, almost jumping with excitement. "The empty vacuum of human experience and our consumer-driven lives. You" – he pointed at Kip – "obviously have an eye for these things." Kip looked torn between confusion and pride at this comment. The man clapped his hands. "Now, I am Mr Jacobsen, your art teacher. Welcome!

Please, everyone, take an easel."

We all moved around and I stood behind my canvas with a feeling of excitement, taking in the fresh pots of paint in every colour, and the long bench that ran down the side of the room, laden with jars of glitter, boxes of charcoal and pastels, and endless packets of pens and crayons.

"What we're going to do today is to create a painting based on your emotional response to this sculpture." Mr Jacobsen gestured towards the toilet rolls. "Please, begin!"

I stood awkwardly in front of my blank canvas. How did the weird sculpture make me feel? Well, confused mostly. All around the room, other students were picking up their paintbrushes. With a shrug I started painting a picture of my confused face. After a while I became totally sucked into the project and I found myself adding other faces to the picture. There was Luigi, with his neat, curling moustache, and Boris, tall and strong like one of those statues of mythical heroes, and Pym, with her bad eye crinkling affectionately.

I was surprised when Mr Jacobsen appeared at my side and pressed a tissue into my hand. I hadn't realized that quiet tears were sliding down my cheeks. I scrubbed my eyes quickly, looking around to check no one else had seen, but everyone seemed focused on their own work.

"It's a powerful thing, art." Mr Jacobsen nodded gently towards my painting. "This is a lovely piece. Full of feelings." I sniffled my thanks and he moved around to where Ingrid was painting.

"What have we here?" said Mr Jacobsen, picking up her canvas and turning it over in his hands. "This is interesting."

"You're holding it upside down," said Ingrid.

"Oh, my apologies," said Mr Jacobsen, turning the canvas around and revealing a painting that was practically a photograph of the sculpture in front of us. "Hmmm," he said softly. "Don't worry, you'll get there."

He drifted over to a very red-faced Kip, who was staring at his own canvas with an angry grimace. "Sorry, sir, I spilled the—" Kip began.

"TREMENDOUS!" cried Mr Jacobsen. "The raw emotion. The passion!" He held out Kip's canvas, on which a large splat of red paint had covered over any of the work Kip had managed to get done.

"Oh, yeah," said Kip quickly. "That's exactly what I was going for. You know, er, passion." Mr Jacobsen nodded seriously and moved along to the next student.

"I think I'm going to like art!" said Kip, beaming at me and Ingrid. Looking at the picture in front of me of my smiling family, I felt exactly the same.

After our lesson I was feeling pretty homesick, but luckily that evening Letty dropped my first letter from the circus on my bed. "I noticed this in your pigeon hole when I picked up my post," she said with a friendly smile. The envelope crackled in my hand as I ripped it open.

Dear Poppy,

Well, it seems funny to write you a letter like this! I'm writing to you from outside the big top and we have just had a great performance. I hope you are settling in well and that you've been putting your friend-making skills to work. I liked the look of that Ingrid girl – a good egg, that one. Everyone is already fighting over who gets to write to you first (and you know what a noisy bunch they are) so I'm going to let them get on with it, but I can't wait to speak soon.

Lots of love,

Pym

P.S. I've enclosed the article we talked about on the phone. This curse business sounds a bit spooky, so be careful!

I WANTED to SAY HELLO POPPY. DON't WORRY. I AM WRITING VERY CAREFULLY tHIS tIME. NO MORE BROKEN PENS FOR M●

What ho, Poppers! It seems that Boris has broken his pen again. Rotten luck, but at least it means I can get a word in. Oh dear, he's making a fuss again. Kicked one of the sandbags right into the air. Chap needs to learn to control himself...Ye Gads! I think it might have hit a cow in the next field. He and Sheila have gone to have a look. At least this time we're not staying next door to an antique china-doll museum. I still see all those glass eyes rolling around on the floor in my nightmares! Those poor, innocent dolls. They didn't stand a chance. Darling Buttercup wants to say hello, but she's just chewing the paper, the scamp. Sorry if it's a bit soggy. I

TOMATO! HELLO. IS ME, FANELLA.
LET ME TELL YOU ABOUT WHAT
THAT BONEHEAD LUIGI DO. WHY HE
LET HIS PRECIOUS BUTTERCUP DO HER
BUSINESS OUTSIDE MY TENT? I ALMOST
FALL OVER IN ALL THIS LION POO. I SEND HIM
TO GET SHOVEL. ME I AM OK, BUT OTIS HE
IS NOT SO GOOD. HE HAS THE UPSET
STOMACH. I THINK HE EAT BOBO'S

BIG SHOE AGAIN. HE IS BIT LUMPY IN THE MIDDLE. AND HE WOULD NOT EAT NICE MOUSE I TRY TO FEED HIM. I GO NOW. I SEE BORIS AND SHEILA COMING UP THE ROAD.

IS THAT A COW?

Me again, Poppy. I'm afraid Boris, Sheila and Fanella seem to be trying to hide a cow inside the human cannon. I'd better go and sort this out.
Lots of love from all of us!

Pym xxx

I read the letter over and over again, tucking the article away to save it for later. Waves of homesickness washed over me, and eventually I fell asleep, Pym's letter still clutched in my hand.

CHAPTER TWELVE

The next morning was Friday and it dawned as bright and sunny as a ukulele song. I knew the artefacts were due to be delivered later on in the day, but I tried to push the thought of them down to the bottom of my regulation white socks and concentrate on the day's lessons.

Ingrid was drifting around our room like a soul headed off to the torture chamber.

"I don't know why they make us take PE," she was grumbling. "What does it have to do with preparing you for the future? I mean, can you imagine going to a job interview? 'Oh, hello, Ingrid, I see you speak seven languages and you have a degree in maths and science and a Nobel Peace Prize, but I'm afraid you can't hit a little ball with a big stick so we're going to have to give the job to someone else.' I mean, REALLY." She huffed and puffed, her face getting redder and her owl eyes getting bigger and bigger.

"Wow, Ingrid," I laughed, "seven languages and a Nobel Peace Prize, eh? Good to see you're keeping your ambitions realistic."

"ARGH. I just HATE it SO MUCH," she howled, ruthlessly tugging her bed sheets into neat corners around her mattress. "I'm so rubbish, and my coordination is terrible."

"I'm sure it won't be so bad," I said, patting her arm. "At least we've got each other. I've never had a PE lesson before." I frowned. "Is it really so terrible?"

"Oh, probably not for you," Ingrid said reluctantly. "It's just bad for people like me with two left feet." I looked down at Ingrid's admittedly quite large feet strapped into her shiny white trainers, but they looked all right to me.

"Well, we'd better get going," said Ingrid with a sigh, her head thrown back as if she was about to walk the plank.

We headed over to the sports hall, where eight other girls were already waiting outside in their PE kits. Unfortunately one of the girls was Annabelle,

121

her silky blonde hair tied up in a navy-blue ribbon. She smirked when she saw us approaching.

"Oh good," she said loudly to the small, dark girl standing next to her, "Ingrid's in our class. At least we know she'll make the rest of us look good." Ingrid's eyes were staring down at her shoes and she was biting her bottom lip very hard.

"HEY—" I started, ready to give this mimsy busybody a good telling off, but I felt Ingrid put her hand on my arm. Miss Reed came jogging around the corner, her ponytail bouncing like a sprightly kangaroo, a shining silver whistle bobbing around her neck and a clipboard in her hand.

"Let's get cracking, shall we?" She pushed open the door to the sports hall and inside I saw that there were thick blue mats on the floor. A gymnastics horse, climbing ropes and a balancing beam were also set up and dotted around. I felt a flutter of excitement, but I was very aware of Ingrid drooping next to me, blinking worriedly at the equipment.

Miss Reed gave two sharp blasts on her whistle and we all shuffled into a tidy line in front of her.

"Hello, ladies." She smiled at us. "And welcome to your first PE lesson. Don't look so nervous; we're going to have a lot of fun together. Now, today is mostly about just taking stock and getting an idea of your different abilities, strengths, what needs work, that sort of thing.

"So," continued Miss Reed, "can I have a volunteer to start on one of the pieces of equipment?"

Annabelle's hand shot up.

"Yes. . .?" Miss Reed looked at her questioningly.

"Annabelle," she chirped.

"Annabelle, thank you." Miss Reed nodded.

Annabelle shot Ingrid a sickly smile, her little eyes snapping nastily. She walked up to the balancing beam and climbed carefully up on top of it. Annabelle stood still for a moment, her eyes screwed up in concentration, and then she turned a neat cartwheel on the beam before jumping off the other end, sticking her bum right out and throwing her arms up high in the air. The other girls gasped, and even I had to admit she had done a pretty good job.

"Excellent, thank you, Annabelle," said Miss Reed, making a mark on her piece of paper. "I see we have some talent here already. Very good work. Now, who would like to go next?"

"Oh, miss," simpered Annabelle lispily, "I'm sure that Ingrid wants to go next; she's *soooo* talented."

She sidled around and pushed Ingrid forward. I didn't have to look at Ingrid to know how horrified she would be, but Miss Reed didn't seem to have noticed.

"OK, wonderful, thank you Ingrid." She smiled.

"NO!" I blurted out, feeling Ingrid quiver next to me. Miss Reed looked at me in surprise. "I mean, I want to go next," I carried on, realizing how rude I sounded. "Umm, please, if it's OK," I finished.

"What an eager bunch!" exclaimed Miss Reed. "Well, if it's all right with Ingrid?" Ingrid nodded gratefully. "OK then, yes, thank you, err. . ." She looked at her list.

"Poppy," I said quietly, "Poppy Pym."

In a daze I walked over to the blue mats. *Just act normally,* the voice inside my head whispered. *Don't draw attention to yourself.* With a sigh I ducked down and did a slightly clumsy forward roll. I heard Annabelle snigger.

"Well," said Miss Reed brightly, "that was a good, solid effort Poppy, thank you."

"Looks like Ingrid's new friend is even worse than she is," I heard Annabelle whisper, and then, making sure Ingrid could hear her, she continued, "and I didn't think it was possible for anyone to be a bigger loser than Ingrid Blammel."

In a flash I saw how hurt Ingrid looked. Annabelle's nasty little smirk swam in front of my face, and I shut my eyes for a second. Then, before anyone could say anything else, I was off. I leapt, I tumbled, I twisted, I sprang into a dizzying combination of backflips, front flips and somersaults. In my mind I could hear Tina and Tawna telling me off:

"No, no, keep your—"

"—back straighter, and don't—"

"—bend your arm like it's a—"

"—chicken wing."

I don't know how long I went on for, it felt like hours, but it must only have been a few seconds. Throwing myself into a full-twisting double layout – where you tumble over and over in the air like a pair of socks in a washing machine – I came to a neat stop, and then, forgetting where I was, I collapsed on to the ground, panting and exhausted. When I sat up, I saw ten faces looking back at me in astonished silence, each one of their mouths set in a surprised pink O. Then, all of a sudden, the silence was broken by Ingrid.

"Yeeeeeeeeeaaaaaaaaaaaaaaaaaaaaaahhhhhhhhhh!!!!" she screeched, pumping her fist up in the air – a most un-Ingrid kind of action. Then all the other girls started cheering, apart from Annabelle, who had her arms crossed and a look of intense dislike burning in her eyes. Miss Reed, looking slightly dazed, was clapping her hands as well and shaking her head. I beamed at them and clambered to my feet.

"Well, Poppy Pym, that was really quite something!" exclaimed Miss Reed.

I shrugged. "Some of it was a bit messy, but it's been so long since I did anything like that without standing on the back of a pony, and the ground just felt so . . . *still*, you know?" I tucked a strand of hair behind my ear.

"A-A pony?" murmured a befuddled-looking Miss Reed, but I didn't have a chance to explain because I was surrounded by the other girls all smacking me on the back and asking me excited questions. I was enjoying myself a lot, until I felt someone pinch my arm fiercely.

"I'll get you for that, Poppy Pym," hissed a voice in my ear, and as I turned and looked into Annabelle Forthington-Smythe's angry blue eyes, I realized that for the first time in my life, I had made an enemy.

CHAPTER THIRTEEN

It seemed that word had got out pretty quickly about my gymnastics escapades. When Ingrid and I walked into our chemistry lesson later that afternoon, the rest of the class huddled around me, talking over one another, and all wanting to know about the circus and what other tricks I could do.

"That is quite enough of THAT." A girlish voice broke through, and everyone whisked themselves back to their seats. There stood Miss Susan. She radiated cleanliness and order, and even the way she moved was neat and precise. She smiled at me, a smile that didn't reach her chilly green eyes. "I see we have something of a celebrity in our midst . . ."

"Sorry, miss, I. . ." I interrupted, about to

apologize and explain, when a curt wave of Miss Susan's very clean hand shut me right up.

"No, thank you, Miss Pym." Miss Susan's emphasis on the P in my name made it sound like an insult. "I don't need to hear your excuses. I would rather not have you waste any more of our time."

My mouth dropped open as she sailed past me to take her place it the front of the class. I shut it pretty sharpish when her gaze snapped on to me again, with a look that made it clear she thought I was some sort of village idiot.

"Right," she trilled with a silvery little laugh that sent a shiver weaselling down my spine, "now that we're all ready to begin. I am Miss Susan, and welcome to your first chemistry lesson of the year." She stood in front of the blackboard with her hands folded together. "Today we are going to be learning about pH values by testing various substances with litmus paper. Now, who can tell me something about pH values?" Her eyes darted around the room before settling on me. "Miss Pym? You seem very fond of the limelight."

"I-I . . . er . . . don't know," I stuttered, feeling my face burning with the fire of a thousand suns.

"Oh, rrrreally," sang Miss Susan, raising one

perfectly arched eyebrow. "How disappointing. Anyone else?"

Surprise, surprise, Annabelle's hand shot up like a jack-in the-box bursting out.

"Ah, Miss Forthington-Smythe," said Miss Susan, her cold smile warming up by several degrees, "would you like to share the answer with the class?"

"Yes, miss," simpered Annabelle, her eyes turned modestly down towards the table as she practically fluttered her eyelashes. "On the pH scale, water is seven, which is neutral. Anything below seven is acidic, and anything above seven is alkaline." She peeped up, smiling sweetly.

"Excellent, well done, precisely right." Miss Susan turned to make a note on the board and Annabelle's smile quickly transformed into a triumphant smirk, which she threw over her shoulder in my direction. Then she whispered something to the girl next to her and they both looked at me and started giggling.

"Now if we could all get in groups and collect our equipment, we'll begin the experiment."

The rest of the lesson seemed endless as my embarrassment made me clumsy, and I bumped into things, almost tripped over Kip, and knocked a measuring jug on to the floor, exploding it into a thousand tiny pieces.

"Oh dear, looks like someone's a bit of a butterfingerrrrrs," trilled Miss Susan, and Annabelle and her friends laughed loudly.

Finally the bell rang, signalling the end of the school day, and I tugged my backpack on, escaping outside as fast as my legs would take me. Kip and Ingrid jogged up behind me.

"WELL . . ." said Ingrid, "what a-a-a . . . nasty lady."

"Ooooh. Harsh words, Ing," joked Kip as he punched me on the shoulder. "Don't let her upset you, Poppy, she was just being a bully. I didn't know any of the pH stuff either."

I gave a watery tortoise smile, and sniffled a bit.

"Anyway," Kip continued, "what's this I hear about you being some secret Olympic gymnast?"

"Ooooooh, Kip." Ingrid turned towards him. "You should have been there. It was amazing. And Annabelle looked like someone had stolen her last cream cake. Especially when she'd just been showing off all her moves." Ingrid stuck her hands in the air and wiggled about until we were all laughing.

"Thank you." I put an arm around each of them. "You're the best. The knees of a bee.

The pyjamas of a cat."

"Yeah, well," said Kip, squirming away from my arm like a worm on a fishing hook, "what I want to know is when you're going to start teaching us some sweet, sweet circus moves!"

"Oh, Poppy." Ingrid turned her moony beam on me with such intensity that her glasses started to steam up. "*Could* you teach us anything?" Her face fell a little, and she twisted a strand of hair around her finger. "Although I'm so clumsy I'm probably a lost cause."

I looked at their expectant faces; Kip was so excited he was swaying back and forth on his heels like a demented rocking horse.

"I suppose I could," I said slowly, thinking about it very hard. "I don't see why we couldn't start some of the basics, anyway. If you really want, I mean."

"YES!" shouted Kip, punching the air.

"Please," said Ingrid more quietly, but with excitement shouting out just as loudly from her eyes.

After dinner we went to one of the common rooms, to sit down and try to mash out some of the details of "Circus School", as Kip insisted on calling it. I suppose you could say that it was our first official meeting, and we talked for a long time, with Ingrid and Kip getting louder and louder and more and more excited.

"How many things can you juggle at once?" asked Ingrid breathlessly.

"Er . . . I don't know," I said honestly, "quite a few, I think. It's harder with wobbly things. I can only manage three bowls of jelly."

"CAN YOU TEACH ME HOW TO WALK A TIGHTROPE? MAYBE WE COULD BUILD A TRAPEZE. OOH, OOH, HOW MANY BACKFLIPS DO YOU THINK I'LL BE ABLE TO DO IN A ROW?" Kip was shouting very loudly, and a girl curled up in a chair in the corner of the room, trying to read a book, was casting extremely dark glares in our direction.

"Calm down, Kip," I grumbled. "For a small boy, you've got a mouth as big as a lion's yawn. Luigi will be wanting to stick his head in it."

Kip grinned, and the three of us all sat around plotting until it had started getting dark outside.

We were interrupted by a loud crunching sound and two beaming headlights creeping towards us. We looked out of the window to see a big truck scrunching slowly up the gravel driveway.

It was here.

A shivery feeling ran up and down my back like a wriggly hamster. We all scrambled outside, just as Miss Baxter emerged from the main entrance and started talking to the two men who jumped down from the truck. Miss Baxter started pointing inside, and soon the men were carrying all sorts of well-wrapped bundles and big crates into the room. Last of all they carefully lowered one huge crate on to a trolley and wheeled it into the building.

"Oh my gosh," squeaked Ingrid, "is that . . . him?"

"Who?" hissed Kip.

"Ankhenamun, of course," I hissed back, my stomach flipping and flopping inside me.

We all jumped back as a sleek black car squealed to a stop right in front of us, spraying bits of gravel everywhere. A very tall and muscly man stepped out. He was wearing a dark suit, and dark glasses that hid his eyes, even though it was dark outside. In his hand was a shining black briefcase, and my breath caught in my throat as I realized the briefcase was handcuffed to his wrist.

"COR!" said Kip, his big voice as subtle as ever. The man peered down at Kip over his glasses, his face a stony mask of displeasure. "I mean, s-s-sorry," he stuttered. The man grunted and, seeing Miss Baxter emerge out of the building once more, headed over to shake her hand. They chatted for a few seconds and then went inside.

"The ruby scarab," muttered Ingrid, shaking her head.

"I can't believe it's really here," I whispered.

And then, with a loud bang, all the lights went out.

CHAPTER FOURTEEN

I stood very still as the darkest darkness smothered itself around me like a thick woollen scarf. There was absolute silence – and then, from inside the school building, came the sounds of lots of people shouting at once. Somewhere, a high-pitched alarm was sounding.

I felt a tug on my arm.

"Poppy?" It was Ingrid, and her voice fluttered out into the night like the nervous wings of a moth.

"Yes," I whispered, "I'm here."

"Must be a power cut," came Kip's too-loud voice, cutting through the air with an edge of nervousness creeping in.

There was a pause.

"That's weird, isn't it," squeaked Ingrid, trying to laugh in a carefree way and failing miserably, "that the power went out just . . . just as the ruby arrived."

The air was warm and soupy, but the three of us stood shivering, straining our eyes and ears for any further peculiar goings-on. In the darkness I began to wish I had taken Pym's advice to eat my carrots a bit more seriously.

There was a rustling noise behind us, and I swung round to find a bright light being shone in my face. I think all three of us screamed then, but it could have been just me, shouting loud enough for three.

"Will you stop that racket?" I heard a cross voice say. It didn't sound like an undead mummy come to eat our brains, but you never know.

"It's Miss Susan," breathed Ingrid, sagging against me in relief.

For a second I thought I'd rather it had been the mummy.

"Yes, it's Miss Susan, and why am I not surprised to find you three lurking about out here when you should be inside?" snapped the chemistry teacher without a trace of her usual frilly voice. She pointed her shining torch away from our faces and towards the ground.

"We were not lurking," I said indignantly, "we just came to see the exhibit arrive and then all the lights went off."

"What are you doing out here, miss?" interrupted Kip.

"That," said Miss Susan, shining her torch in Kip's face, so that he had to scrunch up his eyes, "is absolutely none of your business. Now, let's get you three back inside." And with that she marched off in front, leaving the three of us no choice but to follow in the path carved out by the light from her torch. Was it just my imagination or did Miss Susan seem a bit flustered by Kip's question? My detective senses were tingling, and I could tell a mystery was afoot. (I know I've said it before and so right now in the story you might be doubting my detective skills, but trust me, this time there was actual tingling. I mean, I suppose it could have been the breeze being outside at night, but I'm pretty sure it was detective senses. I'm at least . . . eighty per cent certain.)

Just as we reached the main doors there was a big whooshing sound and all the lights pinged back on, leaving everyone blinking hard at their dazzling brightness.

"Well, that's that sorted anyway." Miss Susan turned off her torch with a sharp click. "Now you lot should be off to your rooms."

"Thanks for looking after us," I muttered.

Miss Susan looked surprised for a second. "Well, that's . . . fine. Now off to bed."

Shouting a quick goodnight to Kip on our way, Ingrid and I legged it back to the girls' dorm and into our room. Letty was nowhere to be seen. I flopped down on to my bed.

"Well, that was all a bit weird," said Ingrid, standing in front of me. "I mean, the power cut and the ruby and everything. You don't think. . ." She paused. "You don't really think it's the curse, do you?"

"No," I said slowly, "but didn't you think Miss Susan was acting a bit funny as well?"

"She's always all stuffy and cross like that," Ingrid answered, moving round to sit on her own bed.

I sat up to face her, and as I did I heard something crunch underneath me. It was the article Pym had sent me inside the letter.

"Oh, I forgot!" I exclaimed. "Pym sent me this. It's that article she was telling me about, you know, the one about the curse."

Ingrid jumped up and came to sit next to me so that we could read the article together. I will stick a copy in right here so that you can see for yourself:

BRILLIANT BEASTS

THE CHILLING CURSE OF THE DOOMED VAN BOTHINGS

BY: MELVYN SPOOKMAN

Here at *Brilliant Beasts and Crazy Curses* we like to bring our readers news of the most terrifying curses to grip the nation, and today's story is no exception. Now, let's delve into the distant past and uncover the horrifying truth behind **the Pharaoh's Curse**. . .

Over three thousand years ago an ancient Egyptian pharaoh placed a powerful curse **(measuring 10/10 on our crazy curse-o-meter!!)** on his favourite ruby beetle. Turns out this Pharaoh's best bud, Ankhenamun, totally murdered him to get his hands on the precious jewel. Unfortunately for Ankhenamun, the curse wasted no time in claiming its first victim . . . him! **(SUCKS TO BE YOU, ANKHENAMUN!!)**

CRAZY CURSES

Fast-forward to two hundred years ago. Lord Anthony Van Bothing, famous Egyptologist, is digging in Egypt when he uncovers Ankhenamun's tomb and finds the ruby beetle tucked away with Ankhenamun's mummified body in his coffin **IN THE PLACE OF HIS HEART!** (That's one cold-hearted dead dude.)

THE CURSE IS RELEASED

Now here's where our story really gets interesting. Six months later, Lord Anthony Van Bothing DIES in a freak **GARDENING** accident. **(ACCIDENT? WE DON'T THINK SO!!)** Death by daffodils? Murder by marigolds? Give us a break! The curse claims another soul, and the bad luck of the Van Bothings is about to become the stuff of legend as tragedy after tragedy STRIKES.

1864. Fifty years later, a fire rips through the Van Bothing estate, claiming the lives of three members of the Van Bothing family, and sixteen servants. The cause of the fire is still unknown, but it is estimated that the fire started in a room that contained NOTHING but a glass display case . . . and inside that case? YOU GUESSED IT! After the fire, the ruby was found in perfect condition, twinkling amidst the embers. **COINCIDENCE?** You decide.

For forty years, its **bloodlust** temporarily satisfied, the ruby sleeps, until a train carrying Lord and Lady Van Bothing jumps the track, crashing in a fiery blaze and leaving their six children **ORPHANED**. From there it's just one "accident" after another.

1914. Three deaths! Patricia Van Bothing crashes her bicycle into a tree, Armand Van Bothing actually slips on a banana peel and falls down the stairs, and Sigmund Van Bothing chokes on a carrot. **A CARROT!!!! ACCIDENTS, OR THE DASTARDLY HAND OF THE PHARAOH'S CURSE AT WORK???**

In 1954, on the same day that his son Percival is born, Lord Alfred Van Bothing dies of scurvy . . . how he got scurvy **NOBODY KNOWS**. (What was he, a pirate??!)

Now, with the sad news that the last remaining member of the Van Bothing family, Sir Percival Van Bothing, has suffered a fatal heart attack, **IS THE CURSE FINALLY BROKEN??** Or is the tormented soul of the pharaoh merely on the lookout for his **NEXT VICTIMS???** We leave it to you, dear reader, to decide.

Ingrid and I finished reading the article, my fingers trembling so hard by the end that the paper was shaking. We looked at each other, eyes as big as frisbees, and suddenly the door to the room swung open with a crash.

There, standing in the doorway, was a small, bald man, and in his hand rested a human skull.

CHAPTER FIFTEEN

"AAAAAAAAAAAAAAAAAAAAAAARRRRRRRR-
RRRRRRRRRRRRRRRRRRRGGGGGGGGGGG-
GGGGGGGGGGGGGGGGGGGGGGGGGGGGGH-
HHHHHHHHHHHHHH!!!!!!!!!!!!!!!!!!!!!!!
!!!" The scream ripped
from me like a sticky plaster from a knee. At my
side, Ingrid was whimpering in fright, as the
figure in the doorway advanced into the room,
the skull in his hand glinting wickedly in the light
from my bedside table. I looked around wildly for
a weapon and seized a hairbrush, which I pointed
with a wobbly hand at the intruder. "Don't come
any closer," I warbled, "or I'll . . . I'll . . . BRUSH
you!"

The figure in the doorway stopped and a curiously girlish voice rang out. "Poppy, what *are* you talking about?"

I lowered my hairbrush, and as the terrifying man moved into the light, I caught my breath. It was Letty! She was wearing a red velvet jacket and she had a swimming cap on her head.

"W-w-what are you wearing, Letty?" I managed. My voice sounded squeezed out of me like the last of the toothpaste.

"It's my costume, dummy. I've been at drama club." Letty pulled the swimming cap off with one hand and her dark curly hair tumbled out around her face.

"What about the skull?!" squeaked Ingrid, looking at the sinister object still resting in Letty's other hand.

"Plastic," said Letty, knocking it against the wall lightly. "We were doing *Hamlet*. You know, ALAS, POOR YORICK." Letty's voice got quite loud and her face started making weird shapes (which is how you tell when someone's acting). She held the skull out in front of her and stared at it moodily.

"Oh, right," I gasped, feeling a bit silly. "I think we're just on edge because of the power cut."

"Yeah! Wasn't it brilliant!" exclaimed Letty. "We had to do a bit of the rehearsal by candlelight and it made it all feel really authentic. It was so creepy. Especially at the start when someone was moving around outside the window with a torch. For a minute we thought it might be a lurking spirit, desperate to return from the afterlife, but then it just went away."

"That must have been Miss Susan," I said thoughtfully. "That's weird. Where were you rehearsing?"

"In the small hall. We were supposed to be next door in the big hall, but the exhibition stuff was turning up so they moved us. There are loads of serious security guards hanging around in black suits. I reckon they must all be spies or something. Anyway, I need to get cleaned up before bed. I've got photography club first thing. . ."

We all got ready for bed, and as I snuggled under my duvet my mind was racing with thoughts of pharaohs and curses and the Van Bothings and a great big sparkling ruby. Eventually my brain wore itself out and I fell dead asleep. (Not *dead* dead, you understand. Otherwise this would be the end of the book and you'd be pretty ticked off because we've hardly even got going on the mystery yet, just you wait.)

The next morning was Saturday and the start of my first weekend at Saint Smithen's. Unfortunately it began with Ingrid and me getting a note to report to Miss Baxter's office. When we arrived outside we found Kip already there, sitting in the waiting area. To one side was a creaking desk covered in paperwork, and sitting behind the desk was Gertrude. Her wrinkled face must have been quite pretty when she was younger, I thought. Under her fluffy grey hair it now looked a bit like an old crumpled apple. She had small pale-blue eyes and a beauty mark buried in the wrinkles of her left cheek. As she gave us a watery smile, she revealed a set of surprisingly white, shiny teeth that looked a bit too big for her mouth.

"Ah, you're all here," she croaked. "I'll go and tell Miss Baxter." And then she hobbled v-e-e-e-e-ry slowly over to Miss Baxter's door and disappeared inside.

"What's this all about?" hissed Kip out the side of his mouth. "What are you two doing here?"

"Dunno," I muttered as Ingrid and I took seats

next to him.

Gertrude came lumbering back out, and gave us another watery smile. "She won't be a minute" she wheezed.

"Thank you," said Kip

"EH?" said Gertrude, cupping her hand around her ear. "What did you say there, young man?"

"THANK YOU!" shouted Kip at the top of his lungs.

Gertrude jumped back a little in shock. "All right, all right, sonny, there's no need to shout." She shuffled back behind her desk and, pulling a big white handkerchief out of her usual crumbly cardigan, she blew her nose noisily.

Miss Baxter stuck her head out of her door. "Ahhh, Kip, Ingrid and Poppy, do come in."

The three of us trooped into Miss Baxter's office and sat across from her on the three chairs she had drawn up in front of her desk. Miss Baxter's big orange cat jumped into my lap and started purring loudly. The gold disc on his collar told me his name was Marmalade.

"Now, I'm sure you know why you're all here. . ." she began. We all shook our heads. "I had a note from Miss Susan, who says that the three of you were . . ." she consulted a piece of paper on her desk ". . . *skulking* around outside last night when you should have been up in your rooms."

"We weren't skulking!" I shouted at the same time as Kip and Ingrid muddled in with their own noisy protests. Marmalade dug his claws into my leg, clearly disapproving of all these noisy children. With a sulky toss of his tail, he jumped down and retired to his usual chair, casting black looks in my direction.

Miss Baxter held up a hand. "Poppy, why don't you tell me what happened."

I looked at the others and they both nodded, Ingrid looking anxious, Kip's mouth set in a hard, angry line.

"We weren't *skulking*," I said. "We were in the common room when we saw the exhibition arrive. We got all excited and we rushed out to see it, and then all the lights went off so we couldn't see anything and we were sort of stuck, you see?" Miss Baxter nodded, so I took a deep breath and continued, "Then Miss Susan appeared with a torch and took us back inside. We didn't even know it was so late, or that we shouldn't have been outside. We're sorry." I finished in a mutter, staring down at my toes.

There was a slight pause before Miss Baxter's smiling voice filled the room up like a warm cup of tea with two sugars. "Well, it seems to me it's all been a bit of a misunderstanding. You must just be more careful in the future. We don't like the students to be outside the front of the school after eight o'clock, but it's for your own safety and so that we know where you are." She looked at our downcast faces and laughed. "Come on, don't be so glum, worse things happen at sea!"

"We didn't mean to," blurted Ingrid.

"It was just really cool," said Kip

"We're sorry," I finished

Miss Baxter stood up. "Well, let's say no more about it. I know that you're all excited about the exhibition, but I hope you know that's no excuse to break the rules." We nodded. "Actually, there's a way you can help me to make up for it." She must have noticed my grumpy face because she laughed and said, "Don't worry, I don't think you'll be too disappointed. I need you to help me take these boxes of brochures down to the main hall. It would take me a few trips, but we should be able to manage between us, and just maybe you'll get a peek at some of the exhibits if they've unpacked things."

With that, any remaining sulks just disappeared and the three of us jumped to our feet.

We followed Miss Baxter down to the doors of the main hall. Two big men in black suits were standing outside, but they waved us through when they saw we were with Miss Baxter. "Just put the boxes down there," she said, and we dropped the boxes by the door.

The room was a mess of crates and packing material. In one corner, a group of people in white coats were huddled around one of the crates having a heated discussion.

". . . and I'm telling YOU, Clarice, that Eye of Horus is clearly seventeenth dynasty!" I heard one red-faced man shout.

"Oh dear," muttered Miss Baxter, "looks like the curators are at it again. . ." She rushed off towards the group, a peacekeeping smile plastered on her face. "Just wait here a moment, you three."

She needn't have said anything because the three of us couldn't have been more glued to the spot if someone had put superglue on the soles of our shoes. In front of us was a small glass cabinet on wooden legs, and inside the cabinet was a green velvet cushion, and on top of that cushion was a brilliant, sparkling ruby beetle.

It was even more beautiful than I had imagined, and as I stood statue still, staring at it with all my might, I felt like I finally understood why Ankhenamun had risked it all – it was glorious. It glittered and dazzled so hard that it almost hurt your eyes to look at it. I looked at Ingrid and Kip's mesmerized faces and I felt mixed-up feelings of fear and excitement spread through my body like a frozen milkshake. The ruby beetle was finally here, and I was more certain than ever that it meant trouble.

CHAPTER SIXTEEN

The rest of the weekend stretched out before us, and of course it was Ingrid who came up with the perfect plan for our Saturday afternoon. Don't ask me how she managed it, but after a short trip to the kitchen, she appeared with an enormous picnic basket in her hand.

"What's in there?" asked Kip, eyeing it hungrily.

"Just some stuff for lunch," Ingrid said. "It says in the handbook that on Saturdays students are allowed to request a packed lunch to eat in the grounds. I thought that as the weather is so nice, we could have a picnic and maybe have the first official meeting of Poppy Pym's Fantabulous Circus School."

"YES!" Kip pumped his fist in the air. "A bucketload of food and some circus tricks. What could be better?"

They both looked at me expectantly. I was a bit nervous about trying to teach someone else my circus tricks because I had never really had to teach anyone anything before. Plus, I still wasn't sure if I should be showing off my circusy-ness. What if Kip and Ingrid thought it was weird, or that I wasn't normal?

"Pleeeease, Poppy?" said Kip in a wheedling voice.

"OK," I said slowly, pushing that worried voice down somewhere deep inside. "Let's do it. It sounds fun."

We took our picnic round to the soft grass at the side of the pond that was marked on the school map. I hadn't been there yet, but it was very beautiful – a big pool of water with a fringe of shady bullrushes lining the edges. A group of fluffy ducklings tumbled along the surface after their bossy mother and it was very quiet apart from the sleepy drone of the dragonflies that flashed blue and brilliant across the water.

"Food first? Or circus?" asked Ingrid.

"FOOD," cried Kip and I in one big hungry voice. Then we watched in wonder as Ingrid unpacked the contents of the basket. There were cheese sandwiches wrapped in waxy white paper, golden-brown mini pork pies, and some flaky sausage rolls still warm from the oven. Ingrid pulled out a big flask and three plastic cups, and finally three giant slices of gooey chocolate cake.

"This can't be what they usually give you for a packed lunch?" I said to Ingrid.

"I just went in and chatted to Mrs Barnfield, the cook," said Ingrid innocently. "She's a nice lady. Collects stamps, you know."

"Ohhhhh." Kip and I shared a knowing look.

"What is this?" I asked, swigging from the drink that Ingrid poured for me. It was spicy, somehow cold and warm at the same time, and the bubbles tickled my nose.

"Ginger beer," laughed Ingrid. "Lashings and lashings of the stuff."

We got to gobbling, and soon only the crumbs of our lunch remained. Kip patted his full stomach with a satisfied smirk on his face. "That was brilliant," he said, lying back on the grass and staring up at the blue sky.

"Really good," I said in a voice full of chocolate cake.

"And now—" said Ingrid.

"—circus time!" finished Kip, bolting up.

"All right, all right, I give up," I said, waving my hands in surrender. "Let's do it."

I made them practise walking up and down in a straight line that we chalked on the tarmac path, and then I strung a low tightrope, just a few centimetres off the ground, between two trees for them to practise on. It took a lot of attempts, but eventually they could both make it from one end to the other without falling off.

"Show us what you can do, Poppy," puffed a pink-faced Ingrid.

"Yeah, go on," came Kip's muffled voice from where he had collapsed, exhausted, on the grass.

I moved the tightrope so that it was a bit higher up, somewhere near my waist, and nimbled across it a few times.

"You're so steady on it!" exclaimed Ingrid.

"You will be too when you've had a bit of practice!" I said reassuringly. "You guys were loads better than I was when I first started."

Kip was sitting on the grass with his arms wrapped around his knees, looking up at me. "Go on, then, clever clogs," he grinned. "Show us a trick."

I walked along to the middle of the tightrope and paused for a moment, breathing deeply and making sure my balance was just right, then in a flash I kicked my feet out from under me, flipping myself forward. I landed on the grass to one side of the tightrope and then sprang up again in one swift motion so that my feet were back on the tightrope and I was standing with my arms held high in the air.

"Wooohoooo!!!" yelled Kip, jumping to his feet. "How long before I can do THAT??!"

"Not long at the rate you're going!" I laughed. "Pym'll be recruiting you to the circus soon."

The three of us went in for dinner, tired and happy. Our first circus class had been a success. Growing up in the circus, I had always been the one being taught, but it felt good to be the one doing the teaching. More importantly, Kip and Ingrid didn't seem to think I was weird at all. In fact, they thought that my circus skills were something special, something they wanted to be a part of. I hugged that thought to myself. It gave me a warm glow in my belly seeing how happy and excited Kip and Ingrid were, and for the rest of the evening there was no more talk of curses or mummies or accidents.

CHAPTER SEVENTEEN

The next afternoon Ingrid and I made our way towards the dining hall to see if we could find something to feed our rumbling stomachs. On our way back through the entrance hall, Ingrid stopped in front of a long wall of small pigeonholes. There was one for each student, with a brass plaque screwed underneath each one with your name on it. Here you might find a note from a teacher or a club organizing an event, or most importantly of all, it was here that your post went here after it had been sorted.

"Hang on a sec," said Ingrid. "The post came yesterday. It should have been sorted by now, and Mum said she'd send me some new books."

Ingrid moved down to one end, pointing her finger along the rows and muttering under her breath. "Berkoff . . . Bhaduri . . . Blammel, here I am!" she exclaimed as she pushed her hand inside the space above her name. When it emerged, her hand was grasping a brown paper envelope and a square of white card. On the card was written: YOU HAVE A PACKAGE WAITING FOR YOU. PLEASE COLLECT FROM GERTRUDE AT RECEPTION.

I felt a fizz of excitement bubble up inside me and went in search of my own tiny postbox. When I found the plaque with POPPY PYM written on it, gleaming away between LARA PUJARI and ANDREW QUEST, I paused for a moment, thinking how strange it seemed to see my name here in this grand building. Looking up at the high, stone ceilings, the fancy iron chandelier, and the big, sweeping staircase, I felt very small, but for the first time I also felt like I was really seeing myself here, like there was a way I could truly be a part of this big, scary school. That feeling rushed like a warm hug from my tingling fingers to my wiggling toes.

Inside my pigeonhole was a card just like Ingrid's, telling me that I had a parcel. I did a little leap for joy, and made the person next to me do a little leap of their own in surprise.

Ingrid and I bustled over to Gertrude's desk quick sharp and joined the queue to collect our packages.

Once Gertrude had thrust an enormous parcel into my arms, I staggered back to the dining hall with it. As they sat around the other tables, loads of kids were excitedly opening their square brown packages and the room was full of jubilant cries like, "RESULT! A giant bag of jelly beans", and heartbroken howls of "NOOOOOO! Raisins again!"

Ingrid was tearing the paper from her own parcel in a mad frenzy.

"YESSSSSSSSSSSS!" she hissed. "The new edition of the complete works of William Shakespeare!" She hugged the book, which was the size of a small dog, to her chest.

"I thought you already had a copy?" I said. "I saw it on your bookcase."

"But THIS one has a new critical introduction," crooned Ingrid, stroking her new pet book tenderly. "It will change EVERYTHING."

I left Ingrid in her cloud of joy and turned my attention to my own parcel. It was huge and square and wrapped in brown parcel paper, just like everyone else's, and I was relieved that my family had done things the same as everyone else for once. I tore the paper away to reveal an enormous cardboard box. I wrestled with the lid for a minute and finally managed to yank it open.

I should have known better.

There was a humongous BANG! and a fountain of glitter and sequins erupted from inside the box, reaching high up, almost to the ceiling. A seemingly endless stream of glitter spewed out of the box; then it drifted down as a glimmering mist, gently covering everything in gold, pink, green and purple sparkles.

I heard a sweet whistling noise and a paper bird rose from the box, flew around the table and then dissolved in the flash of a tiny indoor firework.

I put one sparkling hand to my mouth and peered cautiously over the edge of the box, but was forced to jump straight back when four snakes made of concertinaed paper leapt out and began wriggling across the floor.

I wondered if there was a chance no one had noticed.

Then I looked around, and found myself surrounded by students transformed into piles of glitter, their mouths hanging open. I could feel a deep strawberry blush spreading from top to toe as I tried to stuff things back into the box, but suddenly there was a crackling noise and the room filled with the sound of singing. More precisely, the sound of my family singing. Loudly. "SHE FLIES THROUGH THE AIR WITH THE GREATEST OF EEEEASE, THAT DARING YOUNG GIRL ON THE FLYING TRAPEEEEZE!" I didn't know whether to laugh or cry. I looked over at Ingrid for support, but she was frozen in astonishment just like the others.

"Ahem." I coughed awkwardly into my hand. "Sorry about that."

All at once, the silence broken, it seemed that everyone in the room swarmed forward excitedly, crowding around me and the box and trying to get a look at what was in there.

Inside was a whole range of the finest food the circus has to offer. There were big boxes of different flavoured popcorn, jars of boiled sweets and three big bags of fluffy pink candyfloss. There was also an enormous stash of modelling balloons.

When Miss Baxter walked into the room a few minutes later, I was standing on a chair, making balloon animals. Around me, a crowd of students were shovelling candyfloss into their glitter-smeared faces.

There were shouts of "Now a LION—"

"No, no, a MONKEY—"

"No, no, me next, a PENGUIN!"

I was twisting the balloons as fast as I could, and even though I wasn't a patch on Chuckles and BoBo, I had to say that I thought I was doing a pretty good job.

"CHILDREN!" cried Miss Baxter, looking around her in astonishment. "What on EARTH is going on?!"

Silence fell once more, and the glitter-smeared faces turned towards Miss Baxter. "Poppy?" she asked, looking right at me, a frown appearing between her eyes.

"S-sorry, miss," I said, looking around me at the mess. "It was my parcel. It . . . sort of . . . exploded."

Miss Baxter did not look happy. She clapped her hands together briskly. "Right, everyone get cleaned up and push off. This room needs tidying up before people can eat in it again." All the students began filing out quietly.

"Hang on a minute, Poppy." Miss Baxter placed a gentle hand on my arm. "I would like a word with you."

I hung back, twisting my hands together nervously. Was I about to get in more trouble?

"Now, Poppy. Can you explain what happened, please?" she asked quietly.

"It wasn't my fault!" I burst out. "I just opened the box and all the stuff came bursting out and I couldn't do anything to stop it! I didn't mean to!"

"Right," said Miss Baxter, looking around her at the glitter all over the floor. "I think I had better have a word with your family about appropriate care packages."

"Oh, please don't tell them off," I cried, tears starting in my eyes. "It's not our fault we don't know the rules of this place. It's so big and strange, and everything's so different, and they were just trying to send me something nice."

Miss Baxter stood looking at me for a moment with her arms folded, and then she bent down so that we were face-to-face.

"Oh, Poppy," she said, sympathetically. "I know it all seems a bit odd right now, but you'll get there in the end." She pulled a tissue out of her pocket and handed it to me. "Not everyone has your special talents." She reached down to pick up a balloon kangaroo that I had made and looked at it with a smile. "Like being able to make this, for example. How lovely."

"You . . . you could keep that one, miss." I stammered. "If you like, I mean."

"Thank you, Poppy," she said. "I will put him in my office."

"What about the mess, miss?" I asked, looking around doubtfully at the glitter.

"Well," said Miss Baxter thoughtfully, "while I rather like it, it had better go. I don't suppose there's a hoover in that box of yours? No, I thought not. You'd better run along and find one, then. . ."

CHAPTER EIGHTEEN

It was back to school on Monday and we had our first botany lesson in the greenhouse. Botany is the science of plant life, and Mr Grant, our botany teacher, took it very seriously. One of the great things about Saint Smithen's is that it doesn't just teach the boring old stuff like maths and chemistry that you could learn at any old school. The greenhouse was at the end of the long main building of the school, it was a gigantic round building with a high spherical roof. All of it was made entirely of glass, and it was stuffed with frothy green plants, delicate palm fronds and splashy tropical flowers in every colour of the rainbow. The temperature in there was so hot it made you feel as sticky as a piece of Sellotape and Ingrid's glasses steamed up immediately. Mr Grant himself was a tall black man who wore loose khaki clothes and an explorer hat. Some people said that he had once been a real-life explorer, tearing around in the Amazon, wrestling crocodiles and collecting rare plant samples, and one look at his grizzled face – and the long scar running down his left cheek – was enough to convince me this was true. Despite his fearsome appearance, Mr Grant was softly spoken, and he treated his plants like they were babies.

"Now this here," he said, gently nudging a pretty white snowflake of a flower with his finger, "is an Amazon lily, or *Eucharis grandiflora*, to give it its Latin name. I picked it up last time I was in South America. Note the prominent corona, which is sometimes tinted with green." He gestured to the trumpet shape in the middle of the flower, like the yellow one in the middle of a daffodil. "A very beautiful plant, this one; it likes its shade. Every single part of the plant is highly poisonous if ingested," he added, mildly, as if commenting on the weather. "As with so much in nature, appearances can be deceiving!" He beamed at us all, the long scar on his cheek scrunching up.

"And here" – he continued walking further into the jungley plant life – "are my bees."

We followed him, hearing a low, murmuring buzzing noise. At one end was a glass case with panels of honeycomb inside, and hundreds of bees buzzing all over it. From the glass case, a tube that led outside ran to a hole cut into the glass wall of the greenhouse. It was a clever contraption because it meant the bees could fly out of the hive to collect pollen, but that from the safety of the other side of the glass you could stand right up close and watch the process. We all crowded round to have a look at the bum-wiggling bees.

After a few minutes' lecturing about the bees, it was time to move on, and Mr Grant led us further into the greenhouse, to a couple of tables covered in small black plant pots containing curling green plants.

"Now here," he said, "I have a collection of medicinal herbs. Each one has a reputation for healing in different ways. . ."

I felt a tug on my arm. It was Kip's red-headed pal – the one who had given me the thumbs up in the dining room.

"Psssst," he hissed loudly, clearly sharing in Kip's talent for being quiet and sneaky. Kip and Ingrid turned around too.

"Oh, Ingrid, Poppy, this is Riley," whispered Kip like a booming earthquake.

"Shhhhh!" said Ingrid, panic in her eyes. She cast a sideways glance at Mr Grant, clearly not wanting to get in trouble again.

"Is it true you grew up in a circus?" Riley asked me. I nodded.

Annabelle appeared at Riley's side. "Yeah, Riley, that's why she's so strange," she said, running her eyes over me and making me feel very small.

"Well, I think that is seriously the coolest thing EVER," Riley said loudly.

Mr Grant looked over. "Thank you, Riley, I think so too." He smiled.

Riley blushed and nodded. Then when Mr Grant started talking, he tugged my arm again. "Is it true that you three saw it? The beetle, I mean."

We all nodded.

"Yeah," whispered Kip, "it was so cool. But really spooky."

A little crowd was forming around us; everyone wanted to hear more about the ruby.

171

"What's going on over here, then?" A gentle voice interrupted us, and I turned to find Mr Grant standing right in front of us.

"Sorry, sir," muttered Riley. "It was my fault. I heard that these three" – he pointed at us with his thumb – "saw the ruby scarab this morning and I wanted to ask them about it."

Mr Grant sighed. "And you thought now was the right time to ask? In the middle of a botany lesson?"

"No, sir. Sorry, sir." Riley hung his head.

"Did you, in fact, hear what I had to say about the healing properties of lavender?" Mr Grant asked with a frown.

"N-no, sir," said Riley again.

"I would prefer it if I had your full attention during our time together," said Mr Grant, giving Riley a warning look. "One never knows when this information may come in useful." His frown relaxed into a smile. "Well, now that you *have* asked about the ruby, why don't you tell us a bit more about it, Kip?" he continued. "I myself do love a good ancient artefact . . . I remember one time on the Nile where I had to wrestle an ancient stone out the jaws of an enormous. . ." He trailed off, realizing we were all staring at him, open-mouthed. "Well, anyway." He smiled. "Enough of that, Kip; tell us what it was like."

"It was really cool," said Kip. "Er . . . it was big, and shiny and, er . . . cool."

"Most illuminating, Kip," said Mr Grant, shaking his head.

"Well, I think Ingrid or Poppy could do a better job of explaining, actually," muttered Kip, going a bit pink around the edges.

"It was like magic," breathed Ingrid. "It was all sort of lit up from the inside, and it sparkled in a funny way that made it hard to look at, but at the same time it was really hard to look away. It was smaller than I thought it would be, about the size of a tennis ball, but even then you could see what all the fuss was about – why that Ankhenamun had wanted it so badly." Her huge owl eyes shone like the ruby itself, and I found myself nodding, agreeing with her description.

"It was spooky, like Kip said, though," I added slowly. "Like, it was almost . . . hypnotizing you." I blinked slowly and rubbed my eyes, trying to rub away the feeling that the ruby scarab had stirred up inside me. This time Kip and Ingrid were nodding in agreement.

"Yeah," said Kip, "it's true. You could feel all the . . . oldness." He paused for a second before adding in a quiet voice – almost a whisper: "Like it was . . . the curse."

A gasp went around the room. There had been a lot of talk about the curse buzzing around the school all day, especially after word got out that the power cut had happened just after the ruby entered the building. (A lot of this talk, as you have probably guessed, started with Kip, who played up the moment as dramatically as possible. I even heard someone saying that they'd heard that the second the ruby arrived, lightning had struck the school roof, shutting off all the power, and a ghostly figure had appeared, drifting about screeching, "OOOOO . . . I WANT BRAAAAIIIIINS.")

"Now, Kip," said Mr Grant softly, "I don't think we need to be talking about the curse, do we? After all, we all know curses don't—" He broke off suddenly, tipping his head to one side. "Do you hear that?" he murmured, almost to himself. "It sounds like. . ." Mr Grant's eyes widened underneath the brim of his hat.

We all turned our heads to face the way he was

looking. I could hear a distant humming noise. It was very faint, somewhere near the back of the greenhouse. It almost sounded like. . .

"BEES!" shouted Mr Grant. "The bees are loose! Everyone out! NOW!" and he started hustling everyone towards the door as fast as possible.

Someone screamed and I could hear the buzzing getting louder and louder, a droning sound, thundering and shaking the air around us like when you're near a plane about to take off. I had just been swept through the nearby door with the crowd when I heard a shout. Turning back around, I saw with horror that Kip had fallen over and was lying face down on the floor. I tried to run back, pushing hard against the crowd. I had to go back and get him!

Then, with a horrible creak, the door swung closed.

CHAPTER NINETEEN

"Kiiiiiiiiiiiiiiiiiiiiiiiiiiip!" I wailed. I scrambled over to the door and started wiggling the handle, but it seemed to be stuck. I wrapped both hands around the handle and pulled with all my might but nothing happened. I pressed my ear against the door, trying to hear what was going on inside, but there was total silence.

Suddenly the door swung open, and I went flying backwards. As I soared majestically through the air, I saw Mr Grant emerging at top speed, with Kip tucked up under his arm like a rugby ball. The rumbling, swarming sound of thousands of bees was cut short abruptly as, thankfully, the door slammed shut once more.

Then, THUD! I landed on the floor, and Mr Grant deposited a Kip the colour of skimmed milk on the ground.

"Everyone all right?" he shouted, and then after we all nodded dazedly, he tore off into the distance.

"Kip!" I gasped, rushing over to him. "Are you all right?"

Everyone crowded round to hear what had happened. Kip blinked as if waking up from a deep sleep.

"Yeah," he said slowly, patting his arms and legs as if reassuring himself he was really all there and in one piece. "I don't know what happened. . ." he continued dazedly. "One second I was running, and then I was on the floor, and I could just hear them all getting closer and closer." He paused, his eyes as wide as Ingrid's. "Then Mr Grant was there and he was . . . he was . . ."

"What??!" burst a voice from somewhere in the crowd.

"He was . . . chanting something," said Kip, "and then all the buzzing got sort of quiet and drowsy for a moment, and he scooped me up and then ran out here."

We all stood in silence, digesting what Kip had said.

All of a sudden someone was pushing through the crowd – it was Miss Baxter.

"Hello, Kip, old thing, been having adventures?" Miss Baxter's voice was its usual sunny and relaxed self, but she crouched down and gave Kip a pat on the shoulder. I noticed that Miss Susan was hovering behind Miss Baxter, her eyebrows drawn together in a frown.

"Is that . . . an astronaut??!" Kip squeaked, pointing over Miss Baxter's shoulder. Clearly the shock had been too much for him, poor boy.

But then I saw where he was pointing and, yes, it really did look like an astronaut striding purposefully towards us. He was in a big all-in-one white suit with a helmet. In one hand he was holding a small box, and in the other a flute. As the astronaut waddled closer I could finally see through the mesh covering his face. It was Mr Grant.

"Why is Mr Grant dressed like a spaceman?" I wondered aloud.

"It's a beekeeping suit!" exclaimed Ingrid.

"Everyone all right?" asked a slightly muffled Mr Grant.

"Yes, Michael, everyone seems to be fine. Thank you," said Miss Baxter.

"OK, well, I think it would be best if we cleared the area while I set up the smoke machine," he answered.

"Of course," Miss Baxter replied, pulling Kip to his feet and ushering us all towards the main building.

I, like many of the others, craned my head back over my shoulder for as long as I absolutely could, trying to see what Mr Grant was up to. Finally when we rounded the corner, I asked, "But Miss Baxter, what is Mr Grant actually . . . doing?"

Miss Baxter smiled. "I believe Mr Grant is going to employ some of the skills he learnt from the Bushmen of the Kalahari Desert." Then, laughing at my blank face, she added, "I don't really know an awful lot about it myself, but as I understand it, Mr Grant uses the smoke to calm the bees; then he locates and separates the queen and charms them back into the hive using his flute. Extraordinary, really. Like magic."

I nodded. "Miss Baxter. . ." I began, and then stopped, not quite knowing how to say what was on my mind.

"What is it, Poppy?" she asked gently.

"It's just . . . the power cut . . . and then . . . the

179

bees. You don't think . . . I mean, you don't think it's the . . . the CURSE?" I finished, wildly.

Miss Baxter's face looked very serious for a moment, and she squeezed my shoulder. "No, Poppy, I don't believe in curses, but I do think it's terribly bad luck. I'm also worried about the other students getting scared by this rumour of a curse, so I would prefer it if we didn't discuss it any more." Seeing my disappointed face, she broke into a laugh. "Oh, I know the curse is much more exciting than a coincidence, but unfortunately for us we don't live in a Dougie Valentine mystery, and things here are much more ordinary!"

I nodded, but deep in my heart I knew Miss Baxter was wrong. Hadn't Mr Grant been saying exactly the same thing when a giant swarm of angry bees was released?! It seemed obvious to me that the spirit of the pharaoh was still angry, and my fingers and toes went cold as I remembered what the article had said about the deadly effects it had had on the Van Bothings. Was Saint Smithen's next on the pharaoh's hit list?

Kip, Ingrid and I had arranged to have our next session of circus school that afternoon after lessons had finished. Despite the dramatic morning we'd all had, the sun continued to shine away as though nothing had happened, and we returned to the quiet area next to the pond where we had practised before. Kip and Ingrid had a go at walking the tightrope again, and I even moved it up a few more centimetres because my students were so impressive.

"What about some gymnastics?" asked Kip, a wide smile over his beaming face.

"OK," I said. "How about something like this?" I pushed myself into a neat handstand and then started walking up and down on my hands, my legs stretching straight into the air. Slowly at first, and then faster and faster, I started spinning around and around until I crumpled, laughing, on the ground. Kip and Ingrid clapped and cheered as I pulled myself to my feet and took a wobbly bow. "First," I said, "we have to master the handstand."

It took a long time, but eventually Kip managed to keep himself in a slightly wibbling handstand. Ingrid, on the other hand, just couldn't get her balance, and her face looked decidedly glum.

"Don't worry, Ing," I said, putting an arm around her shoulders, "gymnastics isn't for everyone. That's why there are loads of different people in a circus.

There are lots of other things I can teach you."

"Like what?" asked Ingrid, perking up.

"Like juggling, or making balloon animals, or magic tricks, or—"

"Do you have any books?" she interrupted.

I laughed. "Er, yes, I think I've got one on escapology somewhere back in our room, but I'm not really sure that a book can teach you this kind of stuff."

"Books can teach you *anything*," said Ingrid very seriously. "I've been my mum and dad's accountant since I was seven thanks to *Accounting for Beginners*."

"What's escapology?" Kip interrupted before Ingrid got too excited talking about complicated maths problems.

"It means being able to escape from things," I answered.

"Harry Houdini was a really famous escapologist." added Ingrid. "He was even buried alive a few times."

Kip looked a bit queasy. "Well, I think you'd better read a few more books before you try that one," he said. "Anyway, Poppy, I want to learn a big, proper acrobat trick. Walking on your hands is really cool, but what about some of that tumbling stuff you do? Can't I be part of your routine?"

I frowned. "I don't know, Kip. I think that stuff is a bit tricky. Unless we did something together." I paused thoughtfully. "Tina and Tawna sometimes boost each other into a routine, but I think you have to be quite strong—"

"I can do it!" Kip burst in indignantly. "I'm actually really strong, you know." Then, after a pause: "Um, what would I have to do exactly?"

"You make your hands into a cradle like this." I twisted my fingers together to show him. "And then I put my foot in it. Then you push me up as hard as you can, and it means that I can get much higher and fit an extra twist in while I'm in the air."

"Let's do it!" said Kip, full of gumption.

We tried the trick a few times, but each time I put my weight into Kip's hands we both collapsed into a jumbled heap on the ground.

"This wouldn't be a problem if I was taller," sighed Kip wistfully, rubbing his aching arms.

"We'll get there with a bit of practice," I said.

"Yes," said Ingrid supportively, "on that last one you almost did it perfectly. You know, just before you fell down."

Kip looked a bit cheerier at this, and as the sun

went down the three of us trooped back to the dining hall happy, hungry and full of laughter.

CHAPTER TWENTY

The next day was Tuesday again, and the best day of the week because it was one of the days that I could telephone the circus. I felt like my lessons couldn't go fast enough and impatience pushed up inside me like a helium balloon. One thing that did take my mind off it was my first-ever music lesson. I knew I wasn't very musically talented. Sharp-Eye Sheila had tried to teach me the banjo a few times, but I just couldn't quite get the hang of it. She also tried to teach me how to read music, but it still all looked like a load of sultanas swarming around on a piece of paper to me.

So it was that I approached the music lesson with a faint feeling of dread. That was until I met

Madame Patrice. Madame Patrice didn't just walk into a room, she made an entrance. We were quietly sitting in the classroom when the door swung open with a loud crashing noise and there she stood. Madame Patrice was big and tall. I think she was quite old because her face was covered in wrinkles, but her short, curly hair was a very bright red. She wore a lot of make-up and a long dress covered in bits of lace that looked like it must have once been very grand but was now a bit faded and tatty. Over the top of this was a very long fur stole, and in her hand she held a long black cigarette holder without a cigarette in it.

"Daaaaaaaaaaaaarlings!" she cried in a deep, husky voice.

We all sat open-mouthed and speechless at this dramatic vision of a lady.

She put the empty cigarette holder in her mouth and ran her eyes over us. "There is TALENT in this room," Madame Patrice said, placing a hand over her heart. "I feel it, here. And the heart NEVER lies." With this proclamation she dropped down on to a long red velvet sofa at the front of the room and stretched out a graceful arm. "On top of the piano is some music. Let's hear you all sing together."

We shuffled over to the piano and picked up the music. I couldn't make head or tails of it. There was a long silence and some awkward coughing. Madame Patrice looked at us for a moment.

"I see. You need some encouragement!" And with surprising agility she leapt from the sofa and plonked herself down on the piano stool. Her fingers started crashing down over the keys, and that old machine began to wheeze out a cheerful melody. Madame Patrice's strong, throaty voice soon joined in, singing the song that was written down on the sheet of paper in my hand.

"Now, YOU!" cried Madame Patrice, and she stopped singing.

Quietly at first, but then with more enthusiasm, we all began singing, and Madame Patrice's jolly clanging on the piano was so infectious that soon I found myself joining in loudly. At first the experience was so much fun that I didn't notice it, but gradually I became aware of a loud honking noise. I stopped singing, and slowly, so did the rest of the class, as the honking noise grew louder and louder. It was only when everyone had stopped singing that I realized what the noise was.

It was Kip.

He had his eyes closed and his hands held out, and he looked completely lost in the music. Unfortunately, you could hardly call what was coming out of Kip's mouth "music". It was loud, certainly, and sometimes very flat, and sometimes very squeaky, and often very shouty. Even Madame Patrice's enthusiastic tinkling came to a crashing halt.

Kip opened his eyes and jumped when he saw everyone staring at him.

"What's the matter?" he asked.

There was a moment of silence and then Madame Patrice jumped up and clapped her hands together in a quick, decisive motion. "My dear boy," she said. "You are NOT a singer."

There were a few muffled giggles, and Kip looked a bit upset before Madame Patrice broke in again, her eyes shining. "YOU are a tuba player."

"A-a-a tuba player?!" Kip repeated, wonderingly.

"A tuba player," repeated Madame Patrice firmly, and she moved over to the large store cupboard, which she opened to reveal a jumble of musical instruments. Madame Patrice disappeared inside it for a moment and there were a lot of clunking and smashing noises before she emerged carrying an enormous black case, which she plonked down next to Kip. It was exactly the same size as him.

"Er, thanks," Kip said, eyeing up the huge object.

"It will be splendid," said Madame Patrice serenely. "Now, let us continue with the lesson."

The rest of the day seemed to pass in slow motion as I waited until it was time for my call to the circus. That evening was the last the circus would spend at the Flying Ferret before they moved on to their next venue, and I skipped back to the library, excited to share all my news with the rest of my family. I'll stick in another copy of our actual conversation for you.

Beginning of transcript

Leaky Sue: 'Ello, the Flying Ferret, 'ome of the famous ghost lion.

Me: Hi, Leaky Sue!

Leaky Sue: Poppy!

Me: Did you say something about a – a ghost lion?!

Leaky Sue: (*cackling*) Yes, I'm doing a roaring trade – if you'll excuse the pun – thanks to that bloomin' lion. Seems like the combination of zoo animals and ghosties is just what the tourists like. I'm going to be sorry to see the back of 'er, truth be told.

Me: Oh, right. Well, maybe you could get a different ghostly animal. Something more manageable? A parrot might be good.

Leaky Sue: (*thoughtfully*) A ghost parrot, you say. Hmmm.

Me: Yeah! Then you could teach it to say spooky things!

Leaky Sue: Bloomin' 'eck, you could be on to something there, my girl! Ghost parrot . . . hmmm. I'd only need an 'andkerchief with some 'oles in it.

Scuffling noise

Doris: (*muffled*) That's enough of your caterwauling, Sue, stop hogging the phone! Poppy?

Me: Hello, DoDo!

Doris: Hello, Poppy, love! Don't you mind Sue; we're all wanting to hear your news.

Me: Oh, well, it's all still a bit strange, but I'm feeling a lot better, and

Kip and Ingrid are so great. There's some strange stuff going—

A faint whooshing noise followed by a loud *THWACK!***

Doris: That's wonderful news, dear!

Another whooshing noise. Another *THWACK!***

Me: Errr . . . And how are you all doing?
Doris: Oh, you know, can't complain. We've had a lovely week here, sold-out shows. I knitted a dear little hat for Marvin with flaps to keep his ears warm. And I invented a new high-powered laser. Not a lot new with us.

Whoooooooosh. THWACK!!!**

Poppy: DoDo . . . what's going on?!
Doris: Oh, nothing, love. Sorry, is it making a noise? It's just . . . hang on . . .

Clunking sounds of phone being laid down. Muffled shouting

Leaky Sue: If I've told yer once, I've told yer a THOUSAND times . . . NO KNIFE THROWIN' IN THE SITTING ROOM.

Sharp-Eye Sheila: (*sulkily*) I haven't touched the wallpaper. It's hit the apple every single time.

Doris: That's true, Sue. We haven't made any mess.

Leaky Sue: Well, what d'yer call all them chopped-up apples round yer feet, then?

Doris: But they have to go somewhere when they fall off my head, don't they? Anyway, I'll clean them all up. Actually, Pym gave me a bin bag earlier. She's a knowing one, eh?

Clunking noise

Doris: Hang on, Poppy, Sharp-Eye wants a word with you.

Clunking noise

Sharp-Eye Sheila: All right, Poppy?

Me: Hi, Sharpy!

Sharp-Eye Sheila: Just trying out the new knives while everyone's packing up the equipment.

Me: We had our first music lesson today; you'd have loved it!

Sharp-Eye Sheila: Oh, yes I would, but if your teacher can get you to practise then they'll have done a better job than me!

Me: Not fair! I always practised . . . sort of. I just wasn't any good at the banjo. Or the recorder. Or the triangle.

Sharp-Eye Sheila: Nor the tambourine neither. You're the only person I know who can't master the tambourine.

Me: Well, my friend Kip is even less musical than me and he's going to be a tuba player!

Sharp-Eye Sheila: Wonderful, we could do with a decent brass section. Boris has been coming on lovely on his drums. Apart from he accidentally got a bit excited and bashed one of his cymbals too hard.

Me: Oh jeepers, what happened?

Sharp-Eye Sheila: Dunno. Flew right off in the air like a frisbee. Did hear that a farmer down the road fainted after he saw a spaceship hurtle past his head, but probably not related. . .

Me: Er, no, probably not.

Sharp-Eye Sheila: Hang on, Chuckles is here. He wants the phone.

Clunking noise

Chuckles: (*long silence*)

Me: Thanks, Chuckles, that means a lot.

Clunking noise

Pym: Poppy?

Me: Pym!

Pym: Listen, we have to go, but I had to give you a message first. I've had a vision and it's very important. BEWARE THE EYE.

Me: The eye? What does it mean?

Pym: It is unclear, but just make sure you remember. Watch out for the eye.

End of transcript

The phone cut out with a click and I felt fear snaking down my back and goosebumps covering my arms. What did Pym's warning mean? And was it somehow connected to the Pharaoh's Curse? The night sky was inky dark and I hurried back to the comfortable warm glow of the dorm room as fast as my legs would carry me.

CHAPTER TWENTY-ONE

Everything was quiet for a few more days, but we should have known it could only be so long before the curse reared its ugly head again. Friday morning tumbled in as warm and sleepy as a baby goat. I spent it dragging my feet and sighing hideously because our first lesson of the day was chemistry with Miss Susan. Things had not improved there, and I thought I would rather eat a whole plateful of boiled cabbage than have to endure any more of Miss Susan's snotty remarks or hear her frilly, trilling voice.

"Come on, Pops, it won't be so bad," said Ingrid. "Remember how much I was dreading PE and now I think it's sort of fun. Plus with all this circus training I think my reactions have already improved." She waved her hands as if swinging an imaginary bat.

Even though I knew Ingrid was right, it was still with great reluctance that I shuffled after her towards the lesson. When we arrived, everyone was waiting outside.

"Miss Susan's not in there," said Kip, pointing at the room. "No one is. She must be late."

I pressed my hand against the cool door and it swung open. "Well, it's open," I said.

"We might as well go in and sit down," piped up Annabelle, bossily. "There's no point waiting out here with all the riff-raff," and she looked down her nose at me.

We all grabbed our bags and shuffled in, strangely quiet. It was hard to imagine the super-efficient Miss Susan being late for anything.

"Hellooooooo?" I called, but there was no response. "Maybe she's in the storeroom." I pointed towards the front of the classroom, behind Miss Susan's desk and at the door to a small room where the lab equipment was kept. I walked closer to take a look, calling out again, "Miss Susan? Are you there?" but the door was partly open and it was clear that the room was empty apart from the usual glass beakers and the locked cabinet containing the chemicals.

As I turned back to face everyone, I saw something out the corner of my eye that made my heart trip over itself with a thuddity-thud.

"No, she's not here," I said loudly. "I suppose we might as well all just sit down and wait."

While everyone else was distracted – grumbling, settling in and pulling out their pencil cases – I gestured to Kip and Ingrid. "LOOK!" I hissed out of the side of my mouth, and I pointed to the blackboard. There, drawn in chalk, was a symbol in the shape of an eye. It looked just like an ancient Egyptian hieroglyph!

Nobody else seemed to be paying much attention to it, but then nobody else was on a top sleuthing mission like we were.

"Hmm," muttered Ingrid, her forehead scrunched in concentration. "Curious."

"I think you mean WEIRD," said Kip. "What do you think it means?"

"I don't know," I answered, "but it must have something to do with the curse, don't you think? And why is it in Miss Susan's room? Where *is* she?"

"What are you three doing?" came a shrill voice as Annabelle descended on us.

"None of your beeswax, Annabelle," answered Kip sharply. "Why don't you mind your own business for once?"

"Oooooooh!" smirked Annabelle. "Sorrrrry, Mr High and Mighty. Just looked to me like you might be up to some troublemaking, and as you know I've been made prefect now." She pointed to a shining red-and-gold badge pinned to the front of her shirt. "My daddy joked that it should say 'PERFECT', hahaha!" Annabelle trilled, turning to her appreciative friends.

"Oh yes, Annabelle," breathed Trixie Pepperington-Wallop, one of Annabelle's most annoying sidekicks, "that's sooooo true!"

"Ugh!" interrupted Kip loudly. "Put a sock in it, Trixie. I think we should all just sit down."

We all returned to our seats and waited, a gentle murmur of chatter filling the air.

"Well, I'm the prefect," sang Annabelle in her annoying whine, "and I'm not even sure we should be waiting around much longer for a teacher who can't be bothered to show up. It's disgraceful, really. In fact, my daddy says. . ." Annabelle's tirade was cut short by the appearance of Miss Susan. Was it my imagination or was she wearing the same flustered look I had seen on her face the night of the power cut?

Then, with a jolt, I remembered Pym's warning. BEWARE THE EYE. My stomach started doing its own tumbling routine. "Kip, Ingrid—" I croaked, but Miss Susan's voice cut over mine.

"Yes, that's quite enough, thank you, Annabelle," Miss Susan broke in, her voice as chilly as a double scoop of mint choc chip ice cream. "I apologize for my lateness, class. Let's lose no more time before we get started." She looked about the room, which despite its open window shades was still decidedly gloomy. "And why are you all sitting here in the dark?"

"Didn't know where the light switches were, miss," offered a lanky boy named Tom.

"Hmmph," sighed Miss Susan, "they're right here."

And then everything seemed to go in slow motion.

As Miss Susan flicked the light switch, a spark seemed to flash from behind the storeroom door.

There was a split second of silence followed by a loud shriek of "FIRE!"

Flames were licking around the storeroom door frame, a bright dazzling orange. Our table, though separated from the room by the blackboard, Miss Susan's desk, and a generous amount of floor space, was still the closest one to the fire, and I could already feel the heat from the flames. A roaring sound filled my ears.

The room was filling up with thick black smoke and my ears were ringing. I had always hoped that in a situation like this one I would leap to action like Dougie Valentine and find a way to save the day, but instead it felt like someone had superglued me to my seat, and my brain was full of that crackly white noise you hear when you tune the radio. I realized I could hear lots of people shouting and screaming. Everyone started knocking into one another, pushing to get out.

Miss Susan's voice cut through the chaos. "Everyone out! This way, out here!"

I was coughing, my brain trying to make sense of my surroundings. I found myself looking into the dazed, smudged faces of Ingrid and Kip.

"Are you OK?" I shouted. They both nodded.

"Ingrid got knocked over, but I'm all right," said Kip.

"I told you, I'm fine," said Ingrid.

Then Miss Susan was next to us, her hand surprisingly gentle on my arm. "Are you three OK?" she asked.

"We're fine," I managed, spluttering a little, and I saw a look of relief flit over Miss Susan's face.

"OK, then," she said, putting an arm around my shoulders, "come with me. QUICKLY."

The heat from the flames in the store cupboard was growing more intense, and I could hear the sound of smashing glass behind it as we hurried out the room as fast as our wobbling legs would carry us.

We were outside now and crowds of children were huddled around while teachers desperately tried to get them to line up in their groups so that they could mark them off their registers. The school fire alarm was wailing, and in the distance I could hear the answering wail of sirens drawing closer. From one side of the building a thick cloud of black smoke was billowing.

Miss Baxter appeared in front of us. "Thank heavens you're all OK!" she cried. "Is everyone out?"

"Yes," Miss Susan said with a nod. Her voice was

smooth and calm, but I could see that her hands were trembling.

"We're fine," said Kip reassuringly, and Miss Baxter squeezed his shoulder.

"I think it looks worse than it is," said Miss Susan. "It seems that the fire is contained to the storeroom, but there was a lot of smoke."

"But you're all OK?" asked Miss Baxter, quickly.

"Yes, fine," whispered Ingrid faintly, and then she dropped down, hitting the ground like a sack of potatoes.

CHAPTER TWENTY-TWO

Two hours later Kip and I were sitting in the infirmary next to Ingrid, her face a pale moon against her pillow.

"It's so stupid that I have to stay in bed like this," she grumbled. "I feel fine."

"The doctor said you might have a concussion, because you hit your head when you fell. It's just to be on the safe side." I squeezed her hand.

"So what about the fire? Have they found out what happened?" Ingrid asked.

"There was some kind of gas in the storeroom, and the wiring on one of the lights in there was damaged. The spark from the light being turned on reacted with the gas and caused the fire to start," Kip said. "They've checked everywhere else and it's fine, so they think it must have been something to do with the chemicals not being stored properly. Just a weird accident."

"Yes, another one!" said Ingrid, a flash coming back into her eyes.

"What do you mean?" asked Kip

"I know what she means," I said slowly. "After the power cut and the bees. . ." I shook my head thoughtfully. "It's all just too much of a coincidence." As I said it, I felt like a top detective, about to get cracking on my next big case. I cleared my throat. "You guys, I tried to tell you just before the fire started – when I spoke to Pym on Tuesday she said she had a vision. She said BEWARE THE EYE." There was a pause.

"The symbol on the blackboard," said Ingrid, her eyes widening, "What was that doing there?"

"Yeah . . . that was . . . strange," muttered Kip. "But what are you saying? You think the curse is real?"

There was a loud silence, and I could see the other two were feeling as jumbly inside as I was.

"No," I said, thinking very carefully, trying to keep up with the helter-skelter my brain was on. "These 'accidents' – they're not exactly spooky, are they? I mean, it's not like ghosts appearing or . . . or . . . I don't know, undead mummies or anything is it?"

"But neither were the accidents that the Van Bothings had. . ." said Ingrid, fear in her voice.

"Yeah, true," I said, "but it still feels wrong somehow. I mean, the other things, they all happened to one person. The things happening at Saint Smithen's, well, who's the target? I mean, if it was the curse, wouldn't people be dropping down dead in mysterious circumstances? I don't know, it just doesn't add up."

Kip was nodding slowly. "Poppy's right," he said. "The power cut was one thing, but the bees? We had just walked past them. We were looking right at the glass case and there was no way the bees could get out. Someone must have broken the glass."

"Yeah," I burst in, "and the chemicals all being in the same spot that the light was damaged. That's a big coincidence."

"Especially when the whole science block is completely brand-spanking new, and has only just been built," Ingrid joined in, leaning forward in her bed. "Why would a brand-new wire be damaged?"

"Someone did it deliberately!" exclaimed Kip, jumping to his feet.

I felt the fizz of excitement and fear mixing together inside me like a peanut butter and banana sandwich. I had read enough Dougie Valentine books to know that this was what he called a "gut feeling". I knew Kip was right. Someone had been causing these accidents deliberately. The question was, who?

"I think you're right," said Ingrid, her voice breaking into my thoughts. "Even the power cut could have been caused on purpose." She screwed up her face, and I could almost see the cogs in her brain turning round and round. "Somebody wants everyone to think the curse is real. That's *why* they drew the symbol in the chemistry classroom."

"But who would do it? And why?" Kip echoed my earlier thought, his bewildered face a mirror image of my own.

"You know, " I said, "Miss Susan was outside with a torch when the power went off, and Letty said that the drama club saw someone skulking around with a torch not long before she found us."

"You're right," squeaked Ingrid. "And you know what else, she was there after the bee attack too, standing behind Miss Baxter."

"And *she's the one* who turned on the light switch that started the fire in the first place. The symbol was drawn on the blackboard in her classroom!" rumbled Kip, looking dangerously like he was the one about to explode.

The three of us sat staring at one another, eyes as big as dinner plates.

"But wait." Ingrid frowned. "Why would Miss Susan want people to think the curse was real?"

"BECAUSE SHE WANTS TO STEAL THE RUBY!" shouted Kip, jumping from his seat. "Don't you see?! She was skulking around the exhibit just as it arrived! It's the ruby she's after!"

"But then why is she making all these accidents happen?" I said, shaking my head. "Something just doesn't make sense."

We sat in silence for a moment.

"We need some help," I said finally. "We need a plan to flush out Miss Susan, just like Dougie Valentine would do."

"No one will believe us," said Kip gloomily.

But a tiny bean-sized idea had appeared in my brain, and in a moment it had grown into a huge beanstalk-sized idea. "Leave it to me." I smiled. "I think I know who can help us."

*

Ten minutes later I was back outside Miss Baxter's office. Gertrude was in her usual seat, wearing her usual crumbly cardigan. This time it was purple – or had been once, I think. It was really a kind of brown now, and it had little pearl buttons on. She squinted at me and croaked, "Ah, Miss Pym . . . back again. We're going to have to put your name on one of those seats." I smiled as she let out a wheezy laugh. "I'll just see if the headmistress can see you." Gertrude heaved herself out of her seat and started her painfully slow shuffle towards the office. While she was still making her way to the door, it burst open and Miss Baxter came out.

"Ahh, Gertrude, I wonder if you can get the head of the school board on the phone. . ." Miss Baxter trailed off as she saw me. "Poppy! Is everything all right? Ingrid's OK?" A worried frown appeared between her eyes.

"She's fine, miss," I reassured her. "Actually, I came to see you."

"Oh." Miss Baxter smiled. "Well, I'm a bit busy at the moment, as you can imagine."

"It's quite important, miss," I said quietly.

There was a pause and then Miss Baxter smiled.

"OK, I can spare five minutes. Come in." She held the door to her office open for me and I hurried inside.

"It's about the grand opening party – for the exhibition," I burst out, before Miss Baxter had even reached her seat.

Miss Baxter looked confused. "The grand opening party?" she said. "I hadn't even thought about it. Perhaps we should cancel, what with everything that's going on."

Gertrude, who had at just that moment appeared in the doorway, chimed in, "Might be for the best, Miss Baxter. I've got a lot of people going mad on the phone. All this bloomin' curse business and what not. Wouldn't hurt to push things back a week or two."

"No! You can't," I burst out.

Gertrude turned a pair of angry eyes on me, her wrinkly mouth set in a thin line. "Well, I don't think that's really for you to decide, missy," she said sharply. "Just wanted to let you know that Mr Forthington-Smythe is on the phone for you, Miss Baxter, and very rude he is too!"

Miss Baxter sighed. "Thank you, Gertrude. Tell him I'll call him back." Gertrude waddled out of the room, closing the door behind her.

"Now, Poppy, you were saying . . ."

"Please don't cancel the party, miss!" I said, my hands clasped together in what I hoped was a winning and innocent-looking fashion. "Everyone's looking forward to it *so* much."

"I know, I know, I was looking forward to it too," said Miss Baxter wearily, "but these accidents are terrible. Somebody could have been seriously hurt, and I know that the fire chief and the inspector have given the school the all-clear and the damage is limited to the science block, but the students' safety must come first."

"Well, if the school's just been inspected all over, it can't be much safer, can it?" I pointed out.

"I suppose not," mused Miss Baxter. "You wouldn't like to tell Mr Forthington-Smythe that, would you?"

"Ugh. No, thanks," I said, then quickly added, "It's just that, well . . . if you do decide to go ahead and not disappoint the whole school . . . I had a really good idea."

"Really, Poppy? What idea was that?"

"Well, I was just wondering." I felt suddenly shy, and stood, twisting my foot into the carpet. "Do you have any entertainment booked?"

"Entertainment?" said Miss Baxter faintly, obviously surprised by my question.

"Yes," I said, looking up at her, feeling all the pleading shooting out of my eyes like laser beams. "Because I know this really great circus. . ."

CHAPTER TWENTY-THREE

A few days later I was standing outside Saint Smithen's, dancing from foot to foot with excitement. A fully recovered Ingrid was standing next to me. Talk of the curse still rumbled around the school, largely because the curse had become shorthand among us students for any annoying event. ("I lost my shoe – the curse strikes again." "Cabbage soup for dinner – must be the curse." "Curse this curse, I haven't grown a millimetre!" – I think you can guess who that was.) Kip, Ingrid and I had circus classes most days, and I was impressed by how quickly my star students picked things up. School was going well, the sun was shining, and any moment now, my mad, fab family was going to be tootling up the drive, ready for their big performance at the party tomorrow.

Suddenly, Kip arrived, running so fast his legs seemed to be spinning around like a cartoon character's. "Are they . . . here yet?" he panted, his hands resting on his knees, his face as red as a boiled sweet.

"Does it look like they're here yet?!" asked Ingrid, raising her eyebrows and waving her hands around at the totally empty scene.

I grinned. "Trust me," I said, "you'll know when they're here!"

Kip was still breathing too hard to talk properly, but he squinted and gave me a big thumbs up, so I knew he was OK.

Then, in the distance, I heard the first faint sound of music, familiar music that made my toes tingle, the rolling *oom-pah-pah* of the circus.

AAAAAAAAAAAAAGGGGGGGGGHHHHHH-HH!!!!!!!" a strangled shout exploded from Kip, who was so excited he didn't know what else to do.

And then, there they were, the convoy of trucks and trailers that carried my family. The huge blue truck at the front had a loudspeaker attached to the top, through which the music was blasting, and I knew it was also wired up to a microphone inside. Sure enough, a huge booming voice erupted, "ROLL UP, ROLL UP, COME ONE, COME ALL, TO MADAME PYM'S SPECTACULAR TRAVELLING CIRC— OUCH!" Then there was the sound of a kerfuffle, and some wincingly loud screeching feedback, before a new, distinctly female voice was heard.

"SHUT UP, BORIS. YOU KNOW IS MY TURN. RRRRRROLLLLLL UP, RRRROOOLLLL UP. . . OH, LOOK! IS TOMATO!!!!!" and as it came closer, through the front window of the truck I could see Fanella waving wildly while Boris sat next to her, his arms folded and his bottom lip sticking out like a big baby. As soon as he saw me, though, his face broke into an enormous smile and he started waving as well. Over the top of the huge wheel of the ginormous truck sprang the wildly curly hair and distinctive eyes of Pym, looking even tinier than usual in her great big seat.

With a loud groan the truck came to a halt just in front of us, all the other vehicles crunching up behind. And then everyone was there – Pym, Boris, Fanella, Luigi, Tina and Tawna, The Magnificent Marvin and Doris, Sharp-Eye Sheila,

Chuckles and BoBo – and we were all hugging and laughing, and hugging some more. I introduced everyone to Ingrid and Kip, and it was only then that I noticed that the noisy arrival of my family had brought curious teachers and students alike out into the sunshine to see what was going on.

Always happy to see a crowd, everyone sprang into action. The Magnificent Marvin was moving from person to person, doing sleight-of-hand tricks, pulling lollipops and biscuits out of people's noses. Chuckles was juggling ten juggling balls while asking people to throw in even more objects; so far that made ten juggling balls, a shoe, a watch, a watering can and a bacon sandwich that Chuckles kept taking bites out of every time it went around. BoBo was whipping up balloon models in every shape imaginable, including a pretty impressive balloon version of Mr Grant complete with explorer hat that the man himself seemed especially chuffed with. Madame Patrice had cornered Luigi and was smiling at him like he was the last chocolate in the box. Luigi was nervously running a finger around his collar and he had two bright red lipstick marks on each cheek.

I noticed that Miss Baxter was pushing her way

216

through to the front of the crowds, smiling and laughing as she went, until she arrived where Pym was standing with her arm around my shoulder. Pym stuck her fingers in her mouth and gave a shrill whistle, and everyone fell silent.

"Thank you *so much*, and everyone please join me in welcoming Madame Pym's Spectacular Travelling Circus," cried Miss Baxter, the end of her words being eaten up by greedy, roaring applause, foot-stomping and wolf-whistling from the appreciative crowd. I glowed with pride.

"Now, Madame Pym," continued Miss Baxter more quietly, "I'm sure you'd all like to get settled in before dinner. I'll have Poppy take you around to where you can set up. Poppy, you can have the afternoon off to be with your family – it seems that your brilliant idea of inviting them is proving to be a big hit with your fellow students."

I beamed up at her, and then said hurriedly, "Kip and Ingrid too?" I fixed her with one of my killer pleading looks. ". . . Please?!"

Miss Baxter laughed. "Yes, all right then, Kip and Ingrid too. I should have known better than to try and separate you three." She turned to face the crowd. "Everyone else, back to lessons, please."

A huge groan filled the air. Slowly and reluctantly, people started shuffling back to lessons.

Standing near the front of the crowd I saw Annabelle and her parents, who were visiting for the grand opening. They were filthy rich and donated a lot of money to the school, so I heard. (Mostly in a loud and obnoxious voice from Annabelle herself.) Annabelle's parents were exactly as you might imagine them. Her father was a big man with a red face and a bristling grey moustache. He wore a fancy suit and a heavy, shining gold watch that he waved around a lot while he talked to make sure that you noticed it. Annabelle's mother was a small lady with a red face (although no bristling moustache, as far as I could see!) and sharp blue eyes that looked down a long thin nose. She looked like a boiled sweet. As I walked past them, I heard Annabelle say loudly to her father, "That girl's in my class, Daddy, and she's a total FREAK." My cheeks started to burn, and I turned around to say something to her, but Luigi had beaten me to it.

"Ahhh, Hallo!" said Luigi, smiling his most charming smile at the Forthington-Smythes. "I know you!" Annabelle preened and batted her eyes, happy to be the centre of attention. "I am Lord

218

Reginald Felix Anthony Sylvester Lucas, fourteenth Earl of Burnshire," continued Luigi with a little bow, and Mrs Forthington-Smythe certainly seemed to perk up a bit at that information.

"Of course," boomed Annabelle's father. "Must have met at one of Lady Burnshire's shindigs. Splendid woman," he added in an oily way.

"Yes, Great Aunt Hortence certainly knows how to throw a party," said Luigi with a smirk. "And you are . . . no, don't tell me, Mister . . . Fartington-Smith, isn't it?" I let out a little snort of laughter, and I wasn't the only one. Even Annabelle's friends were trying to hide their sniggers.

"It's Forthington-Smythe," ground out Annabelle's father, in a voice that sounded as cold and prickly as a frozen porcupine.

"Ahhh, yes," said Luigi airily, waving his hand around. "Forgive me. For us, the aristocracy, it is so hard to keep the little people straight in our minds – there are so many of you. Come, Poppy!" And with a flourish Luigi took my arm and we marched off behind Miss Baxter and Pym, leaving Annabelle and her parents gasping for air like goldfishes out of water.

"Brilliant!" I heard Ingrid hiss from behind me. Kip followed behind, walking with Boris. Kip looked up at Boris's towering, muscly body and asked in an awed voice, "How on earth did you get to be so very tall?"

Then, in a very solemn voice, I heard Boris answer. "Sprouts."

CHAPTER TWENTY-FOUR

We made our way down to the dip in the grounds where the circus was to be nestled. In a very short amount of time it was all hustle and bustle down there, as Boris single-handedly put up the big-top tent, lugging tent poles over his shoulders as if they weighed no more than a sack of potatoes. Fanella and Luigi set out the stalls where, before the performance, they would be selling clouds of candyfloss as well as doughnuts, sugary sweets of every colour and size, and swirling lollipops as big as your face. I noticed that Kip was trailing around after Boris with a notepad and pen, asking loud questions like, "AND EXACTLY HOW MANY SPROUTS A DAY ARE WE TALKING HERE??"

Pym pulled me into an enormous and gloriously familiar hug and then stood back, her hands still on my shoulders, as she stared into my eyes with her scrunched-up look. "OK, lovey," she said, "time to tell everyone why they're here."

I stood up in front of the group and started recounting the story from the beginning. I told them about the curse (there were gasps), I told them about the accidents (there were more gasps) and I told them about Miss Susan (there were threats. "You tell me where this Miss Susan sleeps," muttered Fanella, darkly. "Maybe Otis has a little escape. . .").

When I had finished my story, everyone sat very still, apart from The Magnificent Marvin, who jumped up from his seat with a loud, "Yaroooooo!" His eyes were glowing with excitement. "Oh, Poppy, it is just like a Dougie Valentine book!" he cried, accidentally disappearing and reappearing with a loud bang in his excitement.

"I know," I said, nodding seriously, "but what we need to do is to find out for certain who the culprit is. We didn't know what to do, but I was sure that if we all put our brains together we could come up with something. We don't have any proof it was Miss Susan. I suppose we don't even know that it's not the curse after all."

A shiver went around the room. "As to that," said Pym slowly, "I am pretty sure someone just wants you to think that the curse is real. That symbol you described, Poppy, the one that looked like an eye. Well, it sounds to me like that's the Eye of Horus, an ancient Egyptian symbol of *protection*. There's no way that anyone who knew anything about hieroglyphs would draw it somewhere they were trying to cause an accident."

"Yes," said The Magnificent Marvin. "And the fact that someone was skulking around the room with the artefacts during the power cut, which is especially suspect when the ruby had just arrived. It sounds to me like someone's definitely trying to get their hands on the ruby. If you think about it, this curse business is the perfect way to distract everyone."

"But if someone's after the ruby, how do we work out who?" I asked.

Everyone was silent for a moment.

"I don't know, Poppy," said Marvin slowly. "But Dougie Valentine always goes on a fact-finding mission when he's getting stuck into a mystery."

"You're right!" I cried. "We need more information,

and I know just where to gather it . . . at the big party tomorrow night. Everyone will be there, so it's the perfect place for us to do a little spying!"

"But Poppy, you know we're all supposed to be here setting up for the big show. How will we get in unnoticed?" Pym asked. "We're not exactly . . . errr . . . unnoticeable." And she gestured around at the ramshackle group.

There was a brief silence while this sank in.

"We go in disguise," said Fanella majestically. "I wear the false mooostache and nobody know is me. I can talk fancy like Luigi." She made her voice go all deep, "Tally-ho, pip pip, Jolly good show old pea."

"It's old bean, dear," said Doris mildly.

"Pah!" said Fanella. "Peas and beans is all the same."

"Well, we thought it was—"

"—pretty convincing," Tina and Tawna chimed in.

"We could go in disguise too, as—"

"—waitresses. We can balance four trays at a time—"

"—each!" they added.

"Hang about, though," cried Luigi. "If Fanella's

going as me, then who am I going as?"

"You can go as me!" burst in BoBo. "But we'll have to dye your hair pink." She nodded her bright pink head.

"Pink!" Luigi exclaimed. "Perish the thought."

"Pink hair wouldn't suit Luigi's colouring," boomed Boris, slowly and thoughtfully.

Sharp-Eye Sheila nodded briskly. "Orange is what he wants, and a close shave." She brandished her knife. "I can have your face as smooth as a baby's bum in no time."

"I say," said Luigi, looking a bit pale. "I don't really like the sound of this at all." He turned to me. "Love to help, Pops, but orange hair and no moustache . . . it simply won't do."

By this time, Kip and Ingrid had dissolved into giggles. I shot them a stern look.

"Don't worry, Luigi, nobody is going to shave you. Nobody is going in disguise," I said firmly.

There was an enormous groan from the group.

"Not fair," muttered BoBo sulkily.

"I think Poppy's right," said Pym. "We don't want to draw any attention to ourselves and I think even in the *excellent* disguises you have suggested, it would be difficult to extinguish your" – she ran

225

her eyes over the group assembled in front of her –
"originality."

"So it's just us three who are doing the spying,
then?" asked Kip, looking a bit daunted.

"Well," I said, crinkling my nose up as I thought
very hard. "There is a way to get at least one of you
in . . . as a performer!"

"ME!" shouted Marvin. "Oh please, please! I
could do a magic performance and try out my
detective skills."

"A magic performance would be the perfect
cover," chimed in Ingrid. "The Magnificent Marvin
could move around the crowd, asking questions to
the grown-ups that we can't really get away with. . ."

"And Marvin, he can wear the moooostache," said
Fanella graciously.

"I'm not wearing that blimmin' moustache,
Fanella!" Marvin cut in.

"Bah!" scoffed Fanella.

"Anyway, it's a plan!" I interrupted, clapping my
hands triumphantly and stopping the argument
before Fanella could really get going.

"And for my grand finale . . ." said Marvin
dreamily, "I shall make the ruby DISAPPEAR!"

"Yes," said Pym approvingly, "that ought to set the

cat amongst the pigeons. Might ruffle the criminal enough that they betray themselves. You'll have to keep a beady eye out, children," she finished, fixing us with her own beady eye.

"But how will you make the ruby disappear?" asked Kip.

"A good magician never reveals his secrets," said The Magnificent Marvin mysteriously, tapping a finger against the side of his nose. "You'll just have to witness the magic for yourself."

That night, dinner couldn't go fast enough. All around me I saw everyone shovelling food into their faces as if they were in some sort of enormous and very competitive pie-eating contest, all crazy with excitement for the next day and the double whammy of the grand opening and a circus performance. This was especially impressive in Kip's case, as he sat down with a massive plate of sprouts and bravely gulped them down. His eyes were glazed over, and you could tell that with every swallow he was imagining himself getting a tiny bit taller.

I went to bed with a great big smile on my face. Just knowing that my family was close by made me feel safe and happy. The curse, and Miss Susan, and the mystery – none of them mattered as my head hit the pillow. Instead I heard the circus music looping around and around, and dreamed of candyfloss and pretty white ponies.

CHAPTER TWENTY-FIVE

The next day my brain was buzzing noisily with thoughts about the plan we were going to put in action later that evening. I tried to unravel some of the things I was feeling: nervous about something going wrong; thrilled about finally seeing all the artefacts we had been learning about in our classes with Professor Tweep; excited about putting my detective skills to work; and just a little bit scared about seeing the ruby again. No matter how convinced I was that a human hand was at work behind the "accidents" that had been taking place in the school, the memory of the glowing, glittering ruby still gave me the heebie-jeebies.

Eventually, the sun drifted down in the sky like a slowly deflating balloon, and the light began to fade. Ingrid, Letty and I dashed around our room, getting ready for the big party. I was wearing a light green dress that Fanella had chosen for me, because it matched my eyes. I felt like a stick of celery. Ingrid looked nice in a purple, flowery dress, and Letty looked very dramatic in a long red velvet number with sleeves that drifted down to the floor.

"Wow, Letty, you look great!" I said admiringly.

"Thanks," Letty said, tossing her head and squinting dramatically. "I borrowed it from the costume department. Lady Macbeth. I think I've got some fake blood somewhere," she mused.

"No, no," broke in Ingrid, "I think you look lovely just as you are. Both of you," she added with a smile.

"Harrumph," I said in the voice of a girl who knows she looks like a crunchy salad vegetable.

The three of us went downstairs and joined the crowd mingling outside the great hall, where buffet tables full of tasty food had been set up and dashing waiters in black waistcoats were twirling around, balancing trays arrayed with tiny pieces of cheese and glasses of fruit punch. There were lots of people there looking very fancy, including Annabelle's parents. I saw them talking to some of their snooty-looking friends and as we walked past them I heard Annabelle's mother hiss to her husband, "For goodness' sake, straighten your tie, Melvin!"

We lost Letty almost immediately as she waved at a boy who seemed to be wearing a full suit of armour and disappeared off to chat with him. I heard someone shouting my name and spotted Kip and Riley approaching, both looking very smart (and uncomfortable) in shirts and ties.

"There you are," said Kip impatiently, running a finger along the inside of his shirt collar as if trying to stop it from strangling him. "We've been waiting for you. Come on! Let's get in and see the exhibition!"

We started pushing through the sea of people towards the doors to the great hall, which were tantalizingly open. When we reached them we found that the exhibition space itself was actually a bit quieter – everyone else was obviously more worried about stuffing their faces before they tackled the artefacts.

And that, at last, was the moment when we came face-to-face with Ankhenamun. A red velvet rope hung around the brightly painted sarcophagus, and

231

the lid had been removed, displayed next to it in all its glory. As we edged over and peeked cautiously over the edge, my heart was hammering like an overenthusiastic woodpecker.

Ankhenamun lay inside, his shrivelled, bandaged body somehow smaller than I had imagined. I stood looking at him for a moment. It was absolutely cuckoo-pants crazy to think that thousands of years ago, this very body had been behind the robbery that had carried such terrible consequences.

"He's so—" Ingrid said hesitantly.

"Small," said Kip, an edge of disappointment creeping into his voice.

"Yeah, small but scary. Like you!" said Riley, shoving Kip in the shoulder. "Seriously, though, it gives me the creeps. I mean, that's, y'know" – his voice dropped to a whisper – "a dead body."

We all stood and stared for a few more seconds, and then Ingrid said brightly, "Shall we look at something else?" and we all agreed very quickly.

There was loads of really cool stuff displayed in cases around the room. There were pieces of jewellery with beautiful turquoise stones, and small statues of Egyptian gods with animal heads, and wooden chests. It was strange seeing the ordinary objects – like a wooden chair and a funny mirror – that reminded you that these things once belonged to real people just like us, who brushed their hair and had dinner with their families.

"Hey, look at this!" yelled Kip, and we rushed over.

"What?" said Riley.

Ingrid and I shared a secret look, because Kip was standing in front of a cabinet with a sign that said "The Eye of Horus". It contained lots of pieces of gold sculpted into the shape that we had seen written on the blackboard in the chemistry lab.

"Pym was right!" I muttered under my breath.

"What?" said Riley again, looking more and more confused.

"Nothing," I sang quickly, blasting him with a big smile.

Riley's ears turned as red as strawberries. "Y-y-you look nice tonight, Poppy," he finally spluttered.

I narrowed my eyes at him. "Are you making fun of me?" I asked suspiciously.

"N-no!" he exclaimed. "You look really nice. Like a . . . a . . . beautiful grasshopper," he gasped. "Anyway, gotta go . . . oh, look, is that Eddie?!" He swivelled his head around and without another word legged it back out into the crowd. Strange, I thought, spotting Eddie looking at a collection of old coins in the opposite direction to the one Riley had just run off to. I felt my own cheeks going a bit pink and turned round to see Kip looking as if he had just accidentally eaten a worm.

"Shall we go and look at the beetle?" I said quickly.

Two serious-looking security guards stood near the case in dark suits. By now there was a crowd around the glass case in the middle of the room, so it took a few minutes for us to elbow our way through. Once we did I felt my breath stick like a gobstopper in my throat. It was even more beautiful than I had remembered. Its red glow washed over the faces of all those people huddled around the case, lighting them up like ghoulish monsters. I could see from Kip and Ingrid's big round eyes that I wasn't the only one thinking that the ruby was the kind of treasure a lot of people would like to get their mitts on. In silent agreement, we all tore our eyes away and shuffled over to look at a collection of canopic jars. These jars were the ones that contained the organs removed from Ankhenamun, but somehow even these jars of insides seemed less creepy than the dangerous glow of the ruby.

There was a high, pinging noise and I turned around to see Miss Baxter standing nearby, tapping a fork against the glass in her hand.

"Thank you, everyone. Thank you for being here this evening. It's a very special night for Saint Smithen's, and we are honoured to have this amazing collection here even for a short time." Miss Baxter smiled. "I hope that all you students are making the very most of this wonderful opportunity. It's not every day that you get to see such an amazing piece of the past up close like this." There was a little burst of applause, and Miss Baxter's smile grew even bigger. "I know you are all looking forward to the big circus performance later this evening, but now, as a special treat, here is a surprise guest of honour to dazzle and delight you. It is my pleasure to introduce THE MAGNIFICENT MARVIN!"

There was a bright, dazzling flash, a loud *CRACK!* and from nowhere Marvin appeared next to Miss Baxter. He caught my eye and winked. It was time to put the plan into motion!

CHAPTER TWENTY-SIX

As The Magnificent Marvin began his routine, moving through the crowd to stop and chat and perform a trick amidst *oohs* and *ahhs*, I knew I had to track down Miss Susan as quickly as possible. I peered around the room. Eventually I spotted her, and my heart started racing when I realized she was standing next to the very glass case with the ruby beetle in. As I made my way towards her, I spied several other teachers in the room as well: there was Professor Tweep, his walrus face shiny and happy; Miss Baxter was there of course, with Gertrude standing behind wearing her crumpled purple cardigan; Mr Grant was looking sharp and dangerous in his suit; and Dr MacDougal was standing next to Madame Patrice, who was absolutely drowning in sequins. When I reached Miss Susan, she looked down at me, her face flushed. Was it my imagination or was she wearing that nervous look again?

I stared straight ahead, pretending to be watching The Magnificent Marvin pull a canary out of Professor Tweep's mouth. Whenever I felt that Miss Susan's attention was also on the show, I tried to be tricksy, like they are in books, and look at her out the corner of my eye. I don't know if you've ever tried to look at anything out the corner of your eye, but as eyes are round, I think it's a bit of a silly idea, to be honest, and I just stood there, my eyes bulging like daffodil bulbs, giving myself a headache. In the end I had to settle for turning my head and giving Miss Susan lots of little lightning-fast glances. She was wearing a clean white dress and a pretty watch, the band made up of lots of pearls strung together; her hair was pinned up and she even had some make-up on. I had to admit that she looked very pretty, and not at all like her usual frosty self. I also noticed that she had a large black bag at her feet with a corner of crimson material poking out of it. Strange indeed.

I was feeling very proud of my sneaky detective skills when I heard Miss Susan's voice in my ear. "Are you quite all right, Poppy?" she asked. "You seem to have developed a terrible twitch. You're jumping all over the place!"

"Er, yes," I muttered. "I was just wondering if you were enjoying the show?"

Miss Susan looked anxiously at her watch, and answered in a distant-sounding voice, "What? Oh, yes. Very good."

"And now," I heard The Magnificent Marvin boom dramatically as he came closer towards both us and the ruby, "for my grand finale, I will undertake an impossible task. Many of you know the story of the ruby scarab beetle, that it carries an ancient and" – he paused, his eyes wandering around the room – "some say *deadly* curse. You may even think that this curse has been making itself felt even since the ruby reached Saint Smithen's." I looked quickly at Miss Susan's face to see how she reacted to the magician's words. I could see no change in her face, but as The Magnificent Marvin continued to talk, I saw that she once more glanced impatiently at her watch. What was she waiting for?

"—and when they pulled away his bandages what

should they find, in the dried-up chasm of his empty body, in the place of his heart, but this glistening, spectacular ruby?" I was torn away from my own thoughts by The Magnificent Marvin bringing his story to a close. Even though, by now, everyone was familiar with the story of the Pharaoh's Curse, I still felt a collective shiver run around the room, and instinctively I, like many others, turned towards the sarcophagus where Ankhenamun lay – so near and yet so far from his precious ruby.

"Yes," said The Magnificent Marvin solemnly, nodding, "there lies the man himself, a man willing to risk it all, a man willing to *murder*, a man willing to *die* for this beautiful jewel." The magician had the crowd eating out the palm of his hand now, as hundreds of round, goggling eyes stared at the beetle locked in its impenetrable chamber. "And how did he come to possess it?" said The Magnificent Marvin, stroking his chin thoughtfully. "Did he ask for it? No! Was it a gift? No! He took it. He STOLE it." I glanced up at Miss Susan's face again, and this time she was staring intently at The Magnificent Marvin.

"And so, for my final trick this evening, I too will attempt, before your very eyes, to steal this prized artefact from its glass prison." The Magnificent Marvin's voice thundered out, and next to me I heard Miss Susan let out a small gasp. My heart jumped, but I told myself not to get too carried away; after all, a lot of other people had gasped as well. Marvin was doing such a good job.

"But how to go about it?" I heard Marvin muse thoughtfully. "The ruby is protected by an impenetrable glass case, and Miss Baxter tells me the case is alarmed." He looked over towards Miss Baxter, who nodded in agreement. "Perhaps," said Marvin, "I should just . . . take it."

And with that he pushed his fingers against the side of the cabinet. I felt the crowd tense, waiting for the alarm to go off, but it didn't. Then, slowly, miraculously, Marvin's fingertips began to push through the glass. This time it was definitely not only Miss Susan who gasped – everyone did, and then the room fell so silent you could have heard a feather hit the floor. Slowly, slowly, The Magnificent Marvin's whole hand appeared inside the glass case, and his long fingers closed around the ruby.

I held my breath. Even though I had seen Marvin do similar tricks before, I was swept up in the excitement of the crowd. I even forgot about Miss

Susan in that moment. Very carefully Marvin pulled his hand back, through the glass. He lifted his hand high in the air, and there it was, the ruby scarab!

A great big roar of applause burst out and I joined in enthusiastically. Next to me, Miss Susan was clapping too, her eyes sparkling. Marvin held up his hand for silence like the conductor of a great orchestra, and the applause stopped instantly.

"But wait," said The Magnificent Marvin, smiling broadly. "Now, like Ankhenamun, I have a problem. If I wish to keep my treasure, I must make it . . . disappear." I looked at Miss Susan, but this time she was frowning, looking worriedly at her watch again. I couldn't believe it. What on earth was she waiting for?

The Magnificent Marvin held the ruby outstretched in his hand and the crowd swayed forward, their eyes glued to the beetle, all of them under Marvin's spell. All but one. Miss Susan was now shuffling anxiously from foot to foot.

Suddenly there was a bright explosion in Marvin's hand, and when the mist cleared, the ruby had disappeared! The applause welled up again, filling the room like a thunderstorm. I wanted to see if Miss Susan looked worried by the ruby's disappearance, but she was looking down at the floor as she picked up her big black bag.

"But don't worry, Miss Baxter, I am no thief," laughed The Magnificent Marvin. "I only like to borrow these things," and with another golden flash the ruby reappeared inside its case.

"Hooray!" shouted the crowd, clapping and wolf-whistling as The Magnificent Marvin threw his hands up in the air and took a bow.

And then, suddenly, there was another bang, and all the lights went out. The clapping stopped abruptly, and someone near me muttered, "Is this part of the show?" I strained my eyes in the dark, trying to see what was going on, but the soupy darkness was black as black could be. Anxious muttering started to fill the room. Then, as unexpectedly as they had gone off, the lights came back on, and we all stood blinking into the brightness.

Someone let out a short, sharp shriek. "The ruby! It's gone!" And with a feeling of horror creeping over me I realized that The Magnificent Marvin stood once more behind an empty glass case, his own mouth open in disbelief. The ruby was gone. And so was Miss Susan.

CHAPTER TWENTY-SEVEN

I whipped my head from side to side but there was no sign of Miss Susan anywhere. I pushed my way towards Marvin, who was drooping next to the glass case, his mouth moving as if he was trying to find some words but failing miserably. Everything was chaos, with people shouting and pushing. The two security guards were shouting into their walkie-talkies. I managed to get through to Marvin and tugged on his sleeve. He turned to me, his eyes clouded over in a fog of confusion.

"What's going on?!" I yelled over the noise.

"I . . . I . . . I don't know!" Marvin managed to choke out.

We both stared at the empty cabinet in front of

us. I crouched down so that my eyes were level with the case.

"Don't touch anything, Poppy!" hissed Marvin, his mouth clamped in a thin, troubled line. "The police will want to see everything exactly as it is." He pushed his hands through his hair and groaned. "How can it be gone?"

I wasn't touching anything – I was a Dougie Valentine fan, after all, and I knew better than to contaminate the evidence. But then I spied something in the case on the green velvet cushion where the ruby had been resting . . . something small and white and round, something smooth and slightly shiny. . .

"A pearl," I breathed.

"What?" said Marvin, bending down beside me.

"It's a pearl," I said, "on the cushion . . . I've seen it before. . ." I scrunched up my nose, trying hard to remember.

"I can't believe it's gone!" Marvin said again, interrupting my thoughts. "What are we going to do, Poppy?"

"Did you manage to get anything useful while you were performing and chatting with the teachers?" I asked in a whisper.

"Not really," Marvin whispered back. "That Mr Grant seemed a bit nervous, like he wasn't really paying attention, and Professor Tweep started to tell me that the Van Bothings had some sort of family scandal in the past, but that headmistress's assistant interrupted us before he could get to the juicy details."

"Oh," I said, disappointed, "we already know about that anyway, from the article about the curse, all those deaths and accidents."

Our conversation was cut short by the sound of sirens and screeching brakes outside.

A few moments later a man in a creased suit pushed his way into the room.

"I am Detective Inspector Arthur Hartley," he said in a calm, smooth voice that somehow made everyone snap to attention. "If you could all file out into the hallway, please, there are policemen here who will need to take everyone's statements, and I'm afraid you will all have to be searched as a matter of procedure." Everyone started moving out of the room, muttering and whispering to one another. "Apart from you, er" – Inspector Hartley appeared at my side and consulted the notebook in his hand – "Magnificent Marvin. I would like to take your statement myself. And Miss Baxter, could you stay as well?" I hadn't noticed Miss Baxter standing there. Her face was so pale that her freckles stood out like full stops on a page, and her eyes were enormous. She nodded.

I slipped my hand into Marvin's and squeezed it. "I'm staying too," I said, and he looked down at me gratefully.

"And who are you?" asked Inspector Hartley, his sharp grey eyes looking me up and down.

"I'm Poppy Pym," I said, sticking my chin out and trying very hard not to look frightened.

"Poppy is Marvin's ... um. . ." Miss Baxter floundered for a moment.

"She's family," said Marvin quietly.

"Fine," said Inspector Hartley briskly, "she can stay as long as she's quiet." And again he fixed me in the cool stare of his grey eyes, and I felt like he could see right inside me and read my mind. I nodded.

"Now, Mr ... Magnificent," began Inspector Hartley, "I understand that you were performing some kind of magic trick when the ruby disappeared."

Marvin nodded. "Yes, well . . . I had just finished, actually, when all the lights went out. When they came back on the ruby was . . . gone."

"Fine," said the inspector, making a note on his pad, "and during this magic trick, you made the ruby appear and disappear? Is that correct?"

"Yes, it is." Marvin agreed.

"I'm afraid I will need you to tell me how the trick was done." The inspector looked at Marvin steadily from beneath his eyebrows.

Marvin paused for a second and then nodded. "Yes, of course," he said quickly. "This morning I went to see Miss Baxter to talk to her about the trick. I told her that I would need to replace the glass part of the cabinet with one of my own, just before the exhibit opened, but that the alarm could be kept on at all times, apart from when I was performing the trick, and then the alarm would be turned straight back on. It seemed so straightforward . . . I mean, I thought . . . who would steal it while the trick was happening and there were hundreds of people staring at the ruby? I never imagined. . ." He broke off, shaking his head, his hands trembling.

"It's not your fault, Marvin," broke in Miss Baxter, twisting her hands, "it's mine. How could you have foreseen this? I am the one responsible for the collection while it is here at the school. It's all my fault!" Puddles of tears shone in her dark eyes.

Inspector Hartley cleared his throat. "Right, well, before we get ahead of ourselves, I need you to tell me more about this glass case. What's so special about it?"

Marvin wiped his hand across his forehead. "Well, as to that," he said, "I suppose you'll be needing to talk with my wife, Doris. She invented it. But she's out in the grounds with the rest of the circus crew."

"The . . . circus?" said Inspector Hartley, for the first time not looking completely sure of himself.

"Yes," said Marvin. "There was supposed to be a performance in the big top after the speeches here, but that'll all be cancelled now."

"Right," said the inspector, frowning. "Well, carry on about the box, will you? Explain the best you can."

Marvin nodded again. "Like I said, Doris invented it – brilliant, she is." He smiled mistily for a second. "She's a scientist, you see. The box isn't made of glass at all; it's a kind of plastic she invented. It's solid, but if you get it wet, it goes sort of weak and stretchy like cling film. I have a little flask of water in my pocket, and during the trick I pour some on my hand without people noticing. Then I can push through the cabinet, you see. When you pull your hand out, the plastic seals back up without leaving a mark."

"But that's . . . extraordinary!" said Inspector Hartley, his pen flying across the paper.

"Yes," said Marvin, smiling, "she's a genius, my wife – used to work for the government. Still consults sometimes. Very hush-hush, of course," he added, tapping the side of his nose and seeing the inspector's eyes widen.

"And who else knows about this box?" he asked.

"Only me and Doris," said Marvin slowly, "and Miss Baxter, of course. Couldn't have done the trick without explaining it to her first."

"Miss Baxter?" The inspector raised his eyebrows at her, but his face was kind.

She nodded. "Yes, Marvin explained it to me, but I told no one else. Although. . ." she trailed off.

"Yes?" the inspector prodded.

"Well, Doris gave me some papers to look over that explained the process, just to reassure me, you know . . . it was very kind of her. But I'm afraid they were rather scientific and I couldn't make head nor tail of them. In the end, Marvin brought the case to my office and showed me. Like you, I thought it was extraordinary. Like magic, really." Miss Baxter smiled at Marvin and he grinned back.

"And were these papers ever out of your sight?" asked the inspector, snapping everyone back to attention.

"I-I left them on my desk for a few minutes," Miss Baxter said reluctantly, "while I went to the kitchens to check on the food for the event. But like I said, you'd have to be a pretty good scientist to be able to make sense of them in the first place."

"Miss Susan!" I burst in, unable to contain myself any longer.

"Who?" Inspector Hartley turned his frown on me.

"Miss Susan. The chemistry teacher. She could read it," I said quickly.

Inspector Hartley turned to Miss Baxter, who shrugged and then nodded. "Well, yes, I suppose she could. But really, Poppy, why on earth would you think Miss Susan had anything to do with this?"

"I don't think," I yelled, dramatically, "I know! And I can prove it!" I pointed at the case. "Look!"

They all huddled around, looking at where I was pointing.

"What is that?" frowned Miss Baxter.

250

"It's a pearl," I said triumphantly, in my best crime-solving voice, "one which, I deduce, has come from the pearl watch that Miss Susan was wearing this very evening!"

CHAPTER TWENTY-EIGHT

You can imagine my surprise when all that my dramatic announcement received was a mild "I shall look into that" from the inspector.

"I very much doubt that Miss Susan had anything to do with this," said Miss Baxter slowly. "I really don't think—"

I cut her off. "But she disappeared at the same time as the ruby!" I shouted. Were these people blind? I was handing them the criminal on a silver plate and no one seemed to care.

"Thank you, Miss Pym," said the inspector gently. "I will look into it further. Now, it has been a very tense evening; I suggest you go off to bed."

"Yes, Poppy," said Marvin, wrapping me in a hug,

"you go and get some rest. We'll talk about it all in the morning, don't worry."

"But . . . but. . ." I stuttered, furious that no one seemed to be taking my accusation seriously.

"Yes, Poppy," said Miss Baxter firmly and with a slight frown. "Off to bed now, and I don't want to hear any more of this nonsense about Miss Susan."

Reluctantly I trudged from the room. As I was leaving, my keen bat ears overheard the inspector speaking in a low voice to Marvin. "I'm afraid I'm going to have to ask you to remain at the school until we reach some conclusions about the case. We'll need you to come down to the station as well. You were, of course, the last one to handle the ruby. . ."

I felt myself turn hot and cold, and as I emerged into the hallway in which several police officers were still interviewing people, the whole room seemed to spin. Marvin was a suspect, and it was all my fault! I had convinced him to help me flush out the villain and now the police thought that he had stolen the ruby himself!

But amidst my rising panic a feeling of calm descended on me, and my mind became as clear and sharp as a glass of lemonade. If the police weren't going to solve this case, then I, Poppy Pym, would take matters into my own hands. I hurried out into the night. I had to find Ingrid and Kip – there were plans to be made.

We made the most of the chaos caused by the robbery, staying up late to scheme. They had both listened, wide-eyed, when I told them about Miss Susan having left the party so suddenly, and the pearl left behind, matching the ones on Miss Susan's watch. When I got to the bit about the details of the magic trick being indecipherable to anyone who didn't know a lot about science, they were as convinced as I was, and we knew we had to come up with a strategy. It would be dangerous, and it would mean breaking a lot of rules, but we knew what we had to do.

Early the next morning the school was still crawling with police officers and the great hall was marked off with blue-and-white police tape. Ingrid and I crept outside to meet Kip, waiting under one of the big trees in front of the girls' dorms until we heard Kip's signal. The signal had been Kip's idea because, he said, "That's what they always do in the books." Even though we didn't really need a signal in the first place, and Kip's "bird call" sounded more like a cat with the hiccups in the second, I knew what he meant, and it gave me a little thrill of excitement that we were behaving like such top-class detectives. In my mind I was already picturing the celebration when we caught Miss Susan. There would be medals, and a party, and Miss Baxter's smiling round face would say, "How lucky Saint Smithen's is to have a hero like Poppy Pym to save us all!" Unfortunately I was interrupted from this excellent daydream by Annabelle and her friends.

"Oh, look!" sang Annabelle. "There's Poppy Pym. I knew there was something wrong with her. Looks like her weird family are just a bunch of thieves."

Before I could say anything, Ingrid swept forward, her face red and her fists clenched. "YOU TAKE THAT BACK, ANNABELLE," she hissed furiously.

"Oh no." Annabelle batted her eyelashes. "Have I hurt your little friend's feelings? What are you going to do about it, Ingrid? Cry?"

There was a pause and Ingrid's fists unclenched. She smiled. "No, Annabelle. Poppy's worth a hundred of you, so you didn't hurt her feelings and you're not going to make me cry. You're just annoying. Like a fly. A buzzy. Little. Insignificant. Fly." Every word that she spoke was like a needle-sharp jab. "So why don't you just buzz off and irritate someone else," Ingrid finished with a flourish. Annabelle stood silently, her mouth hanging open until Trixie tugged her along by the arm and the group disappeared around the corner.

I wanted to cheer and sing but I turned to Ingrid, wide-eyed. "I can't believe you just said that, Ingrid! You're amazing."

Ingrid smiled at me. "What are best friends for?"

I think I could have cried like a big baby right there and then, but just at that moment Kip arrived, not, like Ingrid and me, in his school uniform, but in what appeared to be a pair of green pyjamas with twigs and leaves stuck to them. He had also painted his face green. Ingrid and I goggled at him.

"What . . . what are you wearing, Kip?" asked Ingrid, faintly.

"It's camouflage, dummy!" said Kip, preening in front of us. "Made it myself . . . sneaky, huh?"

"But, Kip," I said carefully, "what are you going to camouflage with? We're going to be inside."

A look of irritation skipped across Kip's face like a cloud across a green sky. "Oh. Yeah," he said, scratching his head with one of his twigs. "Well, I'll just be . . . an indoor plant or something." His eyes warmed up again. "Yeah, that's it . . . hide in plain sight and all that. Brilliant."

Ingrid rolled her eyes, but I didn't want to waste any more time so I just nodded and we all set off.

I was starting to feel really nervous as we went back inside and wound through the hallways towards Miss Susan's room. Kip kept hugging the walls, trying to look as invisible as a boy dressed as a tree in a girls' dormitory can look. We got to the room and I tapped gently on the door. No answer.

"Good," I said. "She must have gone down to breakfast. She is usually down there by now." I pulled out my hairgrip and was about to use it to pick the lock the way The Magnificent Marvin had taught me to get myself out of a pair of handcuffs during a routine. Instead I found the door was unlocked and with a gentle push it swung open.

The three of us stood very still. "Maybe if it's open that means she's coming back soon. . ." said Ingrid, looking worried.

"We'll just have to be quick," I said with more confidence than I felt, still imagining myself as a hero.

Ingrid and I slipped inside and shut the door. The three of us had already agreed that Kip would wait outside and be the lookout. As soon as the door closed behind us, I knew we had made a terrible mistake. I took one look around Miss Susan's neat and tidy room and felt like we were the criminals. I turned to Ingrid.

"This isn't right," I whispered. "We should just go and talk to the police again."

Ingrid nodded. "Yeah, this feels really bad."

Just as we were about to head back out to the hallway, we heard Kip's loud voice on the other side of the door.

"OH, HI, MISS SUSAN!"

Ingrid and I gasped and looked at each other in horror. What should we do now?

"Kip!" I heard Miss Susan exclaim. "What are you doing here in the girls' dormitory? And why on earth are you dressed like a tree?"

"OH, MISS SUSAN, IT'S YOU, MISS SUSAN OUT HERE RIGHT NOW . . . MISS SUSAN" Kip yelled.

"For heaven's sake, Kip, stop screeching like that and answer me. What are you doing here?"

"WHAT AM I DOING HERE? YES. RIGHT. WHAT AM I DOING HERE? ERRR . . . I AM HERE FOR A VERY GOOD REASON. THAT IS BECAUSE . . . ERRR . . . I'M LOST!"

I smacked the palm of my hand against my forehead. Ingrid and I looked around desperately for somewhere to hide and I spotted a tall wardrobe, which I pointed to. Ingrid nodded.

"NO. WAIT. I'M NOT LOST. I . . . NEED YOUR HELP . . . WITH SOMETHING." I could hear Kip floundering, panicking as he tried to remember the plan to get Miss Susan away from the door.

"Really, Kip," I heard Miss Susan say crossly, "I don't have time for this nonsense right now. Go downstairs and have some breakfast or you'll be late for lessons. Miss Baxter will hear about this."

And as the door handle started to turn, Ingrid and I leapt into the wardrobe, sliding the door closed just as we heard Miss Susan enter the room. I felt Ingrid squeeze my hand. We were trapped!

CHAPTER TWENTY-NINE

From behind the door I could hear Miss Susan moving around the room and humming to herself. It was dark and stuffy inside the wardrobe. I hardly dared to breathe, and from the short, stifled gulping sounds Ingrid was making next to me I could guess that she felt the same way.

I strained my ears and could hear a rustling noise coming from the room outside. Miss Susan stopped humming and I heard her sigh with pleasure. "There you are," she crooned, "my prize!" I felt Ingrid's nails digging into my arm. "Oh, you're so shiny and beautiful," Miss Susan continued, and she sounded so happy. "It's a shame I can't put you out on display, but I must hide you somewhere. Now, where shall

I keep you?" I could hear her moving over to the wardrobe. I screwed my eyes up tight, and by now I could feel Ingrid's fingernails leaving big holes in my arm.

The footsteps stopped in front of the wardrobe, and I knew it was now or never. We had caught the culprit red-handed, and we just needed to get out of this in one piece. As the wardrobe door slid open, I crossed both my fingers, desperately hoping Kip had gone to get Miss Baxter and Inspector Hartley as planned. In one swift move I pushed forward and jumped out, shouting in my best Dougie Valentine voice, "We have you surrounded! Surrender, criminal!"

Miss Susan screamed, jumping back from the wardrobe in shock, and a trembling Ingrid came tumbling out behind me.

We all looked at one another in horror. Miss Susan was obviously horrified because two strange people had just jumped out of her wardrobe, and we were horrified by the dawning realization that what Miss Susan held in her hand was not the ruby scarab. It was a large gold trophy.

With perfect timing the door burst open and there stood Kip, his green face paint smeared, his

261

cheeks puffed out as he tried to catch his breath, and behind him Miss Baxter and Inspector Hartley looking completely horrified as well.

"WHAT is going on??" shouted Miss Susan, clutching her trophy and staring wildly around her.

There was a long and terrible pause, and I felt the blood draining from my face.

"We . . . we thought you had stolen the ruby," I managed, trying very hard to look Miss Susan in the eye as my face went from ghostly white to burning, burning red.

"Me?" Miss Susan looked stunned.

There was a horrible pause.

"It's all been a terrible misunderstanding," said Miss Baxter, disappointment stamped all over her face, "and you children have behaved dreadfully. I am shocked. Shocked! Breaking into a teacher's room, well, it's . . ." She trailed off, and I could hear Ingrid sniffling behind me. I felt sick with shame.

"We . . . we knew it was a bad idea as soon as we walked in . . . the door was open . . . but we . . . we couldn't do it – truly – we were just about to leave when Miss Susan came back. And then we . . . well, we panicked," I stuttered, hanging my head. I couldn't believe any of this was happening.

How could I have done such a terrible thing? With a sinking feeling it dawned on me that I might be expelled, and that worse still, so might Kip and Ingrid. All because of my stupid plan. I had disgraced myself, and worst of all I had dragged the two best and most loyal pals in the world down with me. My stomach churned and my head was spinning.

Miss Susan was still looking at us with a dazed expression. "And why did you think I had stolen the ruby?"

"You disappeared when the ruby did, and you were wearing a pearl watch . . . there was a pearl left behind in the case. And . . . and the plans for the magic trick needed a scientist. And then we heard . . . we heard you talking about your prize. . ." I trailed off, gulping as tears threatened to spill out of my brimming eyes.

Miss Susan went over to a chest of drawers, opened them, and pulled something out. She came back and held the object up. It was her watch, and it was clear there was not a single pearl missing.

"The detective already asked me about my watch this morning and, as you can see, it is all in one piece," she said quietly.

I looked over at Inspector Hartley, who was watching the scene with his eagle eyes, and felt another wave of tears rising inside me. I clenched my fists and dug my fingernails into my palms, determined not to cry in front of him.

"As for where I disappeared to. . ." Miss Susan said slowly.

"Elaine!" interrupted Miss Baxter furiously, and I realized Elaine must be Miss Susan's name. "You don't need to say anything else. It is absolutely nobody's business but your own."

"No, no," said Miss Susan with a wave of her hand. "It is silly to be so secretive about it. I was embarrassed, you see. The truth is . . ." She raised her head, and her pale cheeks were stained red. ". . . I'm a ballroom dancer," she said in a strong, clear voice.

Of all the things I had been expecting her to say, that was not one of them. I felt my mouth drop open. "W-what?" I asked

"I'm a ballroom dancer," she repeated. "Well, technically an amateur. It's a hobby. I sometimes sneak into the gymnasium to practise in the evening – that's where I was coming back from when I found you on the night of the power cut. Last night was the big local competition and we had to leave the exhibition early. Michael . . ." Miss Susan blushed again. ". . . I mean, Mr Grant . . . and I were partners and we won. We won this beautiful trophy." She pointed to the gleaming golden cup. "For the tango," she added, picking up a photo off the night stand. It was Miss Susan and Mr Grant with the trophy, and they were both wearing amazing costumes. I could feel my eyes bulging and my brain spinning around trying to keep up with this new information.

There was another long pause as everyone digested this.

"Well," said Inspector Hartley, sounding suspiciously like he was trying to smother a laugh, "I think I'll be getting back to the crime scene now, as everything here is . . . under control." He and Miss Baxter shared a brief look and then he hurried out into the hall.

Kip shuffled around next to me and Ingrid, and the three of us stood there quaking. *How could we have been so wrong?* I thought, miserably.

"Well, you three, I can't remember a time when I have been angrier. I am bitterly disappointed in you. What do you have to say for yourselves?" Miss Baxter's normally sunny face looked pale and pinched.

265

"Oh, Miss Susan. I'm so sorry!" I burst out. "It was all my fault. All my idea. I dragged them into it. I'm so sorry!" I looked at Ingrid and Kip, feeling the weight of my guilt crushing me like a hat full of rocks.

"No," said Ingrid quietly, "it was all of us. We are very sorry."

"Yes," muttered Kip awkwardly, dragging his eyes up to Miss Susan's face. "Sorry, Miss Susan. We got it all wrong. We just wanted to find the ruby."

"And to help Marvin. To prove he didn't do anything wrong," I said, my eyes pleading with Miss Susan for her understanding.

"Whatever your reasons, this is a very serious offence. We may have to talk about suspension . . . or even worse," said Miss Baxter, shaking her head.

I felt my knees turning to custard, and I thought I was going to drop down right there on the carpet. A few weeks ago the idea of coming to Saint Smithen's had seemed like the worst thing in the world, but now the thought that I might be sent away seemed unbearable. I had found true best friends, and I realized with a jolt that I was enjoying school much more than I had thought possible.

"No," said Miss Susan firmly. "What you did was

terrible" – she looked at all three of us very hard and we nodded – "but I know you were trying to do the right thing. You were trying to help a friend." I felt my heart jump just a little as a tiny scrap of hope appeared. "But unfortunately, trying and doing are not the same things. You didn't do the right thing," Miss Susan continued. "What you did was very wrong, and you must face some kind of punishment."

Again we all nodded eagerly. "Yes, of course, miss," said Ingrid.

"Very well," said Miss Baxter sternly. "Miss Susan has been very generous. But it's detentions for you three for the foreseeable future. Starting tonight in the library. Now, come on." Miss Baxter held the door open and the three of us began to trail out.

I turned back quickly to face Miss Susan. My face and mouth and heart were full of feelings. "I really am so sorry," I said quietly.

Miss Susan gave me a very small smile. "It's OK, Poppy," she sighed without a trace of her frilly voice, "we all do strange things for the people we love." Then the smile vanished and her back stiffened. "Just don't let me ever, EVER catch you doing anything like that again."

CHAPTER THIRTY

By the time we hustled back from lessons, there wasn't time to go down to see my family before reporting to detention. When Ingrid and I rushed back to our room to drop off our school bags, I found a note on my bed.

TOMATO! IS ME, FANELLA.

PYM ASK ME TO WRITE YOU THIS NOTE TO
SAY THAT MARVIN HE IS BACK WITH US AND
OK. I ASK HIM IF POLICE STATION WAS SCARY
BUT HE SAY NO, THEY GIVE HIM TEA AND
BISCUITS AND TALK A BIT ABOUT CRICKET.
I SAY BAH, THIS IS BORING AND THEN HE GET
CROSS FOR NO REASON, SO ALL IS BACK
TO USUAL. HIM AND PYM IS GONE TO TALK
TO THE INSPECTOR AGAIN NOW. WE SAW
MISS BAXTER AND THAT MISS SUSAN THIS
MORNING AND THEY SAID YOU ARE IN BIG
TROUBLE AND HAVE THE DETENTIONS. YOU
CAN COME AND SEE US AFTERWARDS TO TELL
US WHAT HAPPENED. MAYBE I SHOULD HAVE
GIVEN YOU THE MOOOSTACHE?

P.S. THAT MISS SUSAN SHE IS NOT SO BAD.
SHE RECOGNIZE ME FROM MY DANCING DAYS
AND TELL ME I AM HERO. I SAY BAH BUT ALSO
KNOW SHE IS ONLY TELLING THE TRUTH.

At four o'clock on the dot, the three of us reported to the library for what we knew would be the first of many detentions. Even though the memory of that morning still left me burning with shame, I was overwhelmed with the relief of not having got into even bigger trouble. I think all three of us knew that a detention spent shelving books was nowhere near as bad as it could have been. So it was with an almost light heart that I found myself in the cool quiet of the library, unpacking boxes and boxes of local history documents.

Mr Fipps, the librarian, was – as usual – asleep behind his desk, snoring gently. The three of us had been given the task of unpacking, cataloguing and shelving several large boxes of documents relating to the school and the surrounding area. It was actually a pretty interesting job and the boxes contained everything from old maps to diaries to photographs.

"Look at this one!" exclaimed Kip, holding up a very old, brown photograph of Saint Smithen's, with a group of pale, small boys in smart suits lined up outside next to glowering teachers in robes that made them look like sinister bats. "They don't look too happy."

"Add it to that pile, there," said Ingrid, who had

slipped immediately into the role of organizer. Ingrid was in her element surrounded by all these historical papers. "Look, you two!" she exclaimed, her voice squeaking up a notch in excitement. "There's a whole box here with stuff on the Van Bothings!"

Kip's head snapped up, but I stared down at my hands. "I don't think we should be talking about the curse any more," I said in a small mouse voice that I didn't recognize as my own. I could feel the other two looking at me very hard, and I raised my eyes to theirs. "I just feel like I dragged you two into this mess with Miss Susan."

"Oh, shut it, weirdo!" said Kip loudly, a friendly grin on his face. "And stop moping around. We're all in it together. So we caught the wrong person, who cares? That's what *always* happens in the books just before they catch the right person. We've got to keep looking!"

I looked at Kip in astonishment and turned to Ingrid, expecting her to look horrified, but she was nodding as well. "Kip's right," she said, and then laughed at our surprised faces. "Well, it had to happen sooner or later!"

"What's bothering me," I said slowly, "is that pearl. If it didn't come from Miss Susan's watch, then where did it come from?" I could feel something tugging at my memory, like a blackbird pulling on a worm. I had seen something recently, but I couldn't quite put my finger on it. I sighed. Maybe it would come back to me.

I looked up to see Ingrid frowning over something. "What's up, Ing?" I asked.

Ingrid looked up, a frown still scrunched above her eyes. "It's this Van Bothing stuff," she said slowly. "I don't know why, but I think there are things missing from it. These articles have bits blacked out, there's a diary here with a load of pages ripped out of it, and look at this photograph." She held out a small black-and-white photo of a man with a friendly face. "It looks like it's been cut in half, like someone's been taken out of it." Kip and I huddled over the picture and realized that Ingrid was right; the man's arm looked like it was supposed to be around someone else's shoulder – you could just see a tiny bit of it left in the picture, but that person had been cut out.

"Perhaps it got ripped?" I said. "Perhaps the other half is still in the box?" Kip started scrambling around in there, trying to find the remaining piece of the photo.

"No, I don't think so," said Ingrid, running her fingers along the side of the photograph. "The edge is so neat. Like someone deliberately cut it with scissors."

"Whaburhghphthp," came Kip's muffled voice from inside the box, which appeared to be swallowing him whole, his two short legs waving around out of the top. Eventually, after much wriggling, his pink face reappeared.

"What were you saying?" I asked, shaking my head.

Kip held out his hand, and in it was what looked like an old roll of film. "I was saying, look at this! It was buried at the bottom of the box. What is it, d'you reckon?"

Ingrid grabbed it out of Kip's hand. "It's an old roll of microfilm!" she cried; then, seeing our confused faces, she added, "It's like a load of scanned documents – usually newspapers. You just need a machine to project them. My mum and dad use them all the time with their stamps." Ingrid snapped her fingers. "I'm sure I saw one in the photocopying room!"

I looked at Kip and Ingrid's flushed faces and felt the now-familiar thrill of stumbling upon a clue. Somehow this microfilm was connected to the mysterious Van Bothings, and the Van Bothings were connected to the ruby. It seemed to me that lost newspaper articles were just the kind of thing Dougie and Snoops would stumble on to in about chapter thirty of one of their books. "What are we waiting for?!" I cried. "Let's go!"

The three of us crept past Mr Fipps into the small photocopying room behind his desk. In one corner of the room a machine stood under a black cover. Pulling the cover off, Ingrid clapped her hands. "Just like the one my parents have!" she whispered as she carefully started the machine and fed the film into the space at the bottom. Turning on a light in the screen, we saw the first projected image from the film. It was a newspaper article from 1974, nothing very interesting, just a story about a charity auction at the Van Bothing estate. Ingrid began clicking through the images, and as we got near the end of the roll, my heart sank. So this was a dead end too, I thought, just a roll of film someone had left in the box by accident.

But then Kip hissed, "STOP!" and there it was, the picture of the friendly man smiling out at us, right in the middle of the screen. And he did have his arm around someone, a young, pretty woman with dark curly hair. We all huddled around the screen and stared at the picture. There was something so familiar about that woman, I thought. I knew that I had seen her somewhere before.

I started reading what was written under the photograph and it was like my brain was picking up all the jigsaw-puzzle pieces that had been in the wrong places and putting them into the right ones. I noticed a small beauty mark on the woman's left cheek, and I could almost hear the imaginary light bulb ping above my head as I realized who it was.

"Holy baloney," I gasped, "it's Gertrude!"

CHAPTER THIRTY-ONE

"Gertrude?!" cried Kip and Ingrid with one voice.

"Look!" I pointed to the caption underneath the picture. It said:

Sir Percival Van Bothing and his cousin, Gertrude Van Bothing, enjoy an afternoon at the races.

"And look there." I pointed to the picture. "That beauty mark on her cheek . . . the same as Gertrude's!"

"Wait . . . Gertrude? Miss Baxter's assistant?" Kip was looking like someone had smacked him in the face with a wet noodle.

"Yes." I nodded. "It's her."

Ingrid's eyes had sharpened up behind her glasses. "You're right, it does look like her . . . those small eyes, and the dates are right – the picture's nearly forty years old." She shook her head. "But if Gertrude's a Van Bothing, what does it mean? How does that fit into everything?"

My brain was working hard, buzzing and humming like a complicated clockwork contraption – I could feel the cogs whirring as I tried to fit all these clues together.

"Well," I said carefully, "let's look at the facts. For one thing, we know that someone has removed all evidence from the files that Gertrude *is* a Van Bothing. Someone cut her out of that photograph, and pulled out diary pages and newspaper articles that must have mentioned her. They must have missed the roll of microfilm by accident, and if we hadn't found it we'd have no idea."

Something was niggling in my brain, some connection I hadn't made yet. I could feel my mind stretching out for it the way you reach for a lamp in the dark.

"Gertrude must have destroyed all this stuff," Ingrid was saying slowly, "because no one knows who she is, so she must not want them to know. I mean, with the exhibition coming from her family, you'd think she'd have mentioned it. . ."

"But why would Gertrude want to keep her identity a secret?" asked Kip, scratching his head.

"It's about the ruby. I'm sure of it," I said, "She didn't want anyone to suspect she had any connection to it when it went missing. Let me think." I screwed up my eyes as I concentrated hard. An image of Gertrude standing behind Miss Baxter swam into my mind. My stomach did a triple somersault. "Gertrude was there that night." I turned slowly to face Ingrid and Kip, my hands trembling and my heart thumping. "Marvin said she interrupted him and Professor Tweep in a conversation about the Van Bothings. She was wearing that horrible purple cardigan," I whispered, "the one with all the pearl buttons."

We all stood as frozen as ice lollies straight from the freezer. Gertrude had been there. The pearl had been left behind by her. Gertrude had stolen the ruby!

But did she? a tiny, unpleasant voice in my mind asked. *You were wrong before; maybe you're wrong now.* I was all tied up and confused. I didn't know what to think. I remembered how awful it had felt this morning when we accused Miss Susan, and I imagined Miss Baxter's face if we made another mistake.

I turned to Kip and Ingrid. "What do you think?" I asked. "Is it possible? Do you think she did it?"

"Did you see her after the ruby was stolen?" Ingrid asked. "I can't remember seeing her anywhere."

"I can't remember either," I said. "I was so busy looking for Miss Susan, like a complete spoonhead." I smacked the palm of my hand against my forehead. "What are we going to do now?"

"I don't know," said Kip slowly, "but I think we'd better come up with a plan. A better one than last time, anyway. . ." He grinned.

Ingrid was nodding. "I think we should just tell Miss Baxter right away. It's late, but she might still be in her office. She'll know what to do."

"Yes," I said, "and let's take the picture with us. That way we can take it straight down to the circus if Miss Baxter's not in. We need to make sure we can clear Marvin's name and they'll all want to help."

With a snort, Mr Fipps woke up. "Eh? What? Oh, yes, how is it coming, then, you lot?" he blustered, looking at us over the top of his glasses. He looked like a droopy, red-eyed basset hound. "What are you doing in there?" He peered into the photocopying room.

I flashed a warning glance at Kip and Ingrid. "Nothing," I said breezily, "just photocopying some of these documents for the files." I picked up a random stack of papers and waved them in Mr Fipps's direction.

"Hmmph," he grumbled, with a yawn. "All right, then." He looked at his watch. "It's half past five now and you've done enough this evening, but make sure you're back here on time tomorrow night."

We grabbed our stuff and shuffled meekly out before tearing off like racehorses in the direction of Miss Baxter's office.

When we arrived, we were grateful to find Gertrude was not at her desk. It would have been hard to act normal while we suspected her of being a jewel thief.

"Look at this," hissed Kip, picking up a book off Gertrude's desk. It was a book on Ancient Egypt, and as Kip lifted it off the desk, a scrap of paper fell out, covered in drawings of the Eye of Horus.

My eyes widened, and I was relieved to notice Miss Baxter's door was slightly open, a soft light shining out from inside.

"Miss Baxter's in," I said, pointing at the door, the relief filling my voice. "Let's go."

I tapped gently on the door, pushing it open wider with the palm of my hand. "Miss Baxter?" I said quietly. "We're sorry to disturb you, but we need to talk to you about the ruby."

"And Gertrude," said Ingrid, coming in behind me.

"And the Van Bothings," said Kip from behind Ingrid.

And then we all stopped dead, because standing behind the desk was not Miss Baxter, but Gertrude.

Gertrude's eyes glittered in the dimly lit room, as hard and flat as shining pennies. Her usually stooped figure was completely upright, and she looked tall and hawklike. In place of her usual bulky cardigan and baggy, misshapen skirt, she was wearing a black polo neck, a black jacket and black trousers. And there was nothing creaky or shuffling about the way she sprang round in front of the desk.

I gasped, and I heard Ingrid behind me give a small moan of fear, because there in Gertrude's hand, glinting sinisterly against her pale skin, was a gun. And it was pointed right at us.

CHAPTER THIRTY-TWO

"You three! I might have known." Gertrude's voice cracked like a whip through the room, as Kip, Ingrid and I stood paralysed, staring at the gun in her hand. "Luckily, in my line of work you come prepared for these problems. Hands behind your backs!" Tugging back one side of her black jacket, she revealed several sets of shining handcuffs clipped to her belt. With an efficient and well-practised motion she snapped handcuffs on all three of us using only her free hand. "Now get over here." Gertrude gestured with the gun towards the desk and we shuffled over. She moved towards the door until she was standing with her back towards it, the unwavering gun still pointed in our direction. I strained my wrists against

285

the cuffs, desperately wishing I had anything to pick the locks with.

"Y-you stole the ruby," I managed to choke out. I tried to sound brave, even though I had never been more scared in my whole entire life. Not even the first time I did a Russian roll on the trapeze.

"Oh, very clever, Miss Pym," smirked Gertrude. "What was your final clue? Me holding you up at gunpoint?"

"But you're a Van Bothing!" blurted Ingrid. "Why do you need to steal it? Surely the ruby belongs to you now that Sir Percival is dead? We thought he didn't have any family left."

A cruel smile clung to Gertrude's lips. "I see you want the whole story," she said. "Very well. Yes, I am Gertrude Van Bothing." She smiled sinisterly at us again. "Both my parents died when I was very young – the Pharaoh's Curse strikes again!" She let out a short, sharp thunderclap of a laugh. "My aunt raised Percy and me as if we were brother and sister. We had many luxuries, many toys and games, but my favourite thing in the whole world was the ruby beetle. My aunt used to let me sit and play with it, and the way it shone and sparkled it was . . . hypnotizing." Gertrude's face had taken on a dreamy, faraway look. "Nobody else loved it like I did, nobody! It should have been mine!" The dreamy look left Gertrude's eyes and was replaced with a smouldering anger.

"When my aunt died, she left everything to her precious Percy, and I was furious. Hadn't I been like a daughter to her? And didn't I love the ruby better than anyone else? And wasn't I a Van Bothing too? Well, I decided that if no one was going to give me what I wanted, it was time to take it for myself. That nincompoop Percy had no idea what I was up to. He was always so simple and trusting, so stupid." Gertrude's mouth was twisted into a sneer. "So I stole it and I ran away. It was easy. I couldn't believe just how easy it was. And then there I was, and the ruby was mine." Her eyes were shining again now, and they seemed almost to glow the same sinister red as the ruby. Suddenly, her face pinged back like an elastic band into a mask of anger.

"But somehow, Percy found me, he tracked me down, and he took back what was mine." Her voice got louder. "MINE. I managed to escape before he could turn me over to the police, but it didn't stop Percy from disowning me, wiping my name from the Van Bothing family tree and pretending I had never existed. That snake! Now my need for the ruby was like a thirst I couldn't quench. I knew I couldn't get my hands on the ruby, but I thought maybe a different jewel would do. It started small: a diamond necklace here, a pair of earrings there, but none of them did the trick. I travelled the globe, and I stole some of the most famous jewels in the world, but nothing compared to my ruby. At night it was like I could hear it calling to me, missing me as I was missing it, longing for us to be together. . ." She broke off with another sharp bark of laughter.

"Oh, yes," she said musingly. "I've done it all in my day – museum busts, bank jobs, the lot. It was . . . *easy* . . . so very, very easy. . ." Gertrude trailed off, lost in the memory of her daring heists.

She's mad, I thought desperately. *She's a crunchy peanut butter nut*. I started trying to look around desperately for an escape, but the only way out was the door behind Gertrude. She was enjoying herself now as she continued her story.

"I got good at being invisible, at blending in, especially as I got older. Nobody ever noticed the little old lady in the background. And then, one day, I heard that Percy had died and I thought, now, now I will get what's rightfully mine." Gertrude rubbed her hands together gleefully. "And when I heard that the artefacts were going to be in a school for six weeks before they moved to the British Museum, I saw my window of opportunity." She looked at us. "It's much trickier, you know, to steal from a museum. Tricky, but not impossible." Her eyes glazed over and a smile played across her face as she obviously remembered other museum-based jewel-stealing capers.

"I got a job as Miss Baxter's assistant, and I thought the rest was going to be a piece of cake, but things were more difficult than I had anticipated. . ."

"The curse," I whispered. "All the accidents. That was you?"

Gertrude let out that short bark of laughter again. "Oh, the curse! Yes, that was a stroke of luck. When I staged that power cut so I could swipe the ruby, I was unlucky that that jumped-up security guard hung around talking with Miss Baxter. And then that horrible little drama group spotted my torch and I knew I had to make a quick getaway and try again. What I hadn't counted on was all the talk of the curse. I knew with a little imagination I could turn that to my advantage. At first I thought a little commotion might pull the guards away, but unfortunately Miss Baxter had actually hired a fairly decent security firm. Of course, they were still no match for me." She smirked wolfishly. "I needed more time to plan, and I thought if I got people riled up enough about the curse, then Miss Baxter would cancel the grand opening and delay things for a while – long enough for me to find a way past her security measures. And she was just about to do it before YOU convinced her not to." She turned her glowing eyes on me.

"But . . . the bees and the fire," I cried. "You could have really hurt someone!"

Gertrude shrugged. "Who cares? If one of you little runts had got really hurt it would only have made the talk of the curse grow stronger, and created enough chaos for me to steal the ruby."

"You're mad!" burst out Kip.

"Mad, am I?" mused Gertrude, pointing the gun in his direction. "Well, maybe I am. But now I have the ruby, finally, all to myself. I just needed to hang around long enough to pin the crime on someone else so I could make a clean getaway. I thought that Miss Susan would be a good candidate, but once again your meddling put an end to that. Now I think your precious Miss Baxter could benefit from a spell in prison!"

"No!" I shouted. "You can't do that!"

"Why do you think I'm in here, snot rag?" chuckled Gertrude. "A few forged letters, some well-placed fingerprints I've collected, and a broken pearl bracelet . . . well, that stupid inspector will have her behind bars by morning."

I knew I had to keep her talking. I cast a desperate look at Kip and Ingrid, but they were both as still as statues, eyes enormous in their pale faces. Then I noticed that Ingrid's hands were moving behind her back. I saw her manage to pull something out of her back pocket – it was a paper clip! The one that Pym had given her weeks ago, when she dropped me off at Saint Smithen's. To my surprise, Ingrid began picking the lock on her handcuffs with nimble fingers. I had to keep Gertrude distracted.

"So how did you do it? Steal the ruby, I mean?" I asked her, trying to keep the trembles out of my voice.

"Nothing could be simpler," smirked Gertrude. "For once your interfering helped me out. By organizing for that group of freaks to come and perform, you gave me the perfect cover. I stood outside this office and heard every word that magician said about how the trick worked." With the tiniest click Ingrid's handcuffs came undone and she slipped them in her back pocket. She shuffled a bit closer to Kip, so that their shoulders were touching. From where Gertrude stood it must have looked as if Ingrid was leaning on him for support, but she was actually busy picking the lock on Kip's handcuffs like a pro.

"So what happened next?" I asked loudly, keeping Gertrude's eyes on me.

"Then all I had to do was set a fuse to blow at the right moment, reach in, and grab my prize." Gertrude put her hand in her pocket and pulled out the ruby beetle. Its flaming glow bounced, reflected a thousand times around the room, lighting Gertrude's face a monstrous red. I felt Kip slip the paper clip into my hand and in a jiffy I was free of my cuffs as well. But it was already too late.

Gertrude gazed lovingly at the ruby for a moment before slipping it back in her pocket. Then she cocked the gun with a terrifyingly clear CLICK.

"And now" – she smiled horribly – "I think it's time for the curse to claim three more victims."

CHAPTER THIRTY-THREE

"Wait!" I shouted, staring down the barrel of Gertrude's gun. "Think about what you're doing! If you shoot us, it won't look like an accident." I darted a look at Kip and Ingrid. "People will be looking for the shooter."

Gertrude clucked her tongue in annoyance and dropped the gun slightly. "Drat!" she muttered. "I hadn't considered that." She looked over at us beadily. "But something must be done about you."

"Perhaps you could leave us here while you escape," said Ingrid quickly. "You could lock us in. No one would find us until you were long gone."

Gertrude tipped her head to one side thoughtfully,

and then her eyes narrowed. "And have everyone out looking for me?" She shook her head. "No, no, no." She tapped a finger against her cheek. "You have to be silenced for good."

I could feel my knees wibbling beneath me as I tried to think clearly. In a flash of extraordinary kid-detective brilliance, a plan appeared in my mind.

"What we need is another tragic accident," Gertrude said slowly, casting her eyes around the room.

"What?" I said loudly. "You want us to take a TUMBLE?" I looked wildly at Kip and Ingrid. Ingrid frowned thoughtfully, but Kip looked horrified.

"Eh?" said Gertrude, temporarily thrown.

"You think Kip and I will FLIP out?" I said, and Ingrid's eyes cleared. She gave me the tiniest of nods. Kip, however, was still looking at me like I had grown an extra arm.

"Stop talking gibberish! Ahhh, I know, a fire would be just the thing." The evil glint was back in Gertrude's eye as she continued to make her dastardly plans. "So sad, such a tragedy, but then you three do have a habit of being in the wrong place at the wrong time. . ." Gertrude started cackling the sort of mad, witchy laugh you expect to hear at Halloween.

I was starting to feel desperate, but I broke in again. "That idea must have given you quite a BOOST." I glanced wide-eyed at Kip in time to see realization spreading across his face like jam across toast. Gertrude, however, was still looking pleased with herself.

"If you start a fire in here, how will you pin things on Miss Baxter?" I said quickly. "All your plans will be for nothing."

"Pipe down, weasel chops!" commanded Gertrude haughtily. Then she let out another little laugh. "There are plenty of ways for me to cast the blame on to your beloved Miss Baxter, don't you worry about that. Anyway, with a blazing inferno like the one you're going to be trapped in, panic about the curse will be stronger than ever! Perhaps I should draw some more of those Egyptian symbolybobs around again, just to get everyone really stirred up. . ."

My heart thudded down somewhere in my shoes.

"So it was you who drew the symbol on the blackboard, then?" asked Kip loudly.

She swung her furious gaze around to Kip's face. "Yes, of course it was me." She sniffed. "I had hoped that little stunt would be enough to fuel talk of the curse and get the opening cancelled, or at least to keep interfering eyes on Miss Susan, especially when I distracted her so that she'd miss the start of the lesson. Of course you morons were meant to turn the lights on before she got there, which would have made her look even guiltier, but yet again you foiled my plans."

Ingrid cleared her throat. "Miss Van Bothing," Ingrid simpered, "I can't tell you how impressive you are."

"Eh?" Gertrude looked at Ingrid, startled.

"Yes," continued Ingrid breezily, "for years now I've been considering how exotic and exciting it would be to be a master criminal." She let out a tiny sigh. "But for us youngsters it's so hard to find a role model, especially one with your flair and talent."

Gertrude preened, but kept the gun firmly focused on us.

"You're just so clever," Ingrid pressed on. "The way you planned it all, the way you tricked everyone . . . it's amazing."

"Well, thank you," said Gertrude, looking pleased with herself, her grip on the gun seeming to relax slightly. "I must say, it's nice to hear from a fan. In my line of work, of course, you don't get a lot of praise, on account of how everybody's so busy trying to find you so they can stuff you in prison."

Ingrid's huge eyes shone with sympathy. "Well, they're the ones who deserve to be locked up – not recognizing a talent like yours. It's criminal!"

Gertrude was nodding eagerly, her gaze fixed, as if hypnotized, on Ingrid, her grip slackening even more so that the gun was now pointing much lower.

"NOW!" I heard Kip hiss in my ear.

And it was different to all those times we had practised it and failed. Kip dropped to one knee, and I stuck one foot in his cradled hands and sprang up with all my might as I felt Kip push me into the air with a strength that even he didn't know he had. I squeezed my eyes closed as Kip's boost sent me spinning up and across the room. In my mind I could see it all happening in slow motion, when in reality it must have taken a fraction of a second. I spun once, twice, and then stretched my legs out straight, feeling the soles of my feet make contact with Gertrude's body.

The sheer force of my kick sent us both crashing along the floor. Gertrude's back and head smacked against the door, and the gun skittered over the carpet. Kip charged towards it as fast as his legs would carry him. Gertrude howled, and I felt her bony hands closing around my throat. I tried to scream, but I couldn't make a sound. I clawed at her surprisingly strong arms, but the world was starting to look as if I was seeing it through a misted-up bathroom mirror.

"YOU MAGGOT! YOU WORM!" screeched Gertrude somewhere above me.

Suddenly there was a loud thunking noise, and, miraculously, I felt Gertrude's hands let go of my throat and flop limply at her sides. Looking up, I saw Ingrid, her eyes blazing fiercely, and in her hands was the heavy book she had just whacked Gertrude on the head with.

I lay on the floor, gasping to get my breath back, as Ingrid and Kip kneeled down beside me.

And then, with a crash, the door to Miss Baxter's office burst open, knocking over the now unconscious Gertrude, and I found myself looking into the worried faces of Pym, Miss Baxter and Inspector Hartley.

"About time you got here," I croaked, and then, very gracefully, I passed out.

CHAPTER THIRTY-FOUR

When I came to, it was to find the anxious faces of Pym and Miss Baxter looming over me.

"Oh, thank goodness you're awake!" said Miss Baxter.

"Hello, lovey, don't worry, you're all right now," murmured Pym, squeezing my hand tightly.

"She's up!" I heard Ingrid shout, and then she and Kip were at my side as well.

I struggled up, feeling a bit stiff and sore but otherwise fine. "Where's Gertrude?" I asked quickly, looking around and realizing I was still in Miss Baxter's office.

"Inspector Hartley arrested her!" Ingrid said quickly.

"Yeah, Poppy, it was so cool. It's a shame you were

all conked out 'cos you'd have really loved it," said Kip enthusiastically, hopping from one leg to the other.

"He will be back in a minute, once he's seen to everything, and I'm sure he'll be able to answer all your questions," said Miss Baxter, smiling. "Although I must say, I'm more interested in hearing your story. What on earth happened?"

And while I sat and sipped a glass of water, the three of us told Pym and Miss Baxter how the events had unfolded. As we were telling the story, I felt like we really were in a Dougie Valentine book, but when I thought about Gertrude pointing that gun at us I began to think for the first time that life inside a Dougie Valentine novel might not be all it's cracked up to be.

Miss Baxter's face was pale by the end of the story, and her voice shook as she said, "I just can't believe all this time it was Gertrude! That little old lady. . ."

We were so wrapped up in the story that we hadn't noticed the inspector slipping back in. "Gertrude's no ordinary little old lady," he said, shaking his head. "She's Light-Fingered Trudy, one of the most notorious jewel thieves in the world, and until five minutes ago she was at the top of the government's most-wanted list for years!" Inspector

Hartley grinned. "You three might have just pulled off the capture of the century!"

"YEAH!" shouted Kip, while Ingrid smiled vaguely. I just felt dizzy with relief that it was all over.

"How did you find us, anyway?" I asked.

"We were with Pym when she had a premonition that you were in trouble," said Miss Baxter. "It was quite extraordinary. Arthur . . . I mean, Inspector Hartley . . . and I went down there to ask some questions." Miss Baxter's cheeks turned pink underneath her freckles. I looked at Inspector Hartley and he quickly hid a smile with his hand.

"I knew something was wrong," Pym put her arm around my shoulders and squeezed me tightly. "I'd been having confusing visions all afternoon. We all came over as fast as we could."

"Well, I'm glad you did," I said, "although Ingrid seemed to have it all under control. Ingrid! How did you know how to get out of those handcuffs like that?"

Now it was Ingrid's turn to blush. "It was all in that escapology book you gave me. And they were only standard chain nickel handcuffs." She shrugged modestly. "It was easy."

"Yeah, and Ingrid knocked that crazy lady out

like she was some kind of ninja!" Kip shouted. "And Poppy and me did our trick perfectly. I knew I was strong enough—" Kip broke off as though struck by an important thought. "The sprouts," he whispered. "The power of the sprouts is real."

"Well, I think all three of you displayed great bravery, and proved to be top-class detectives even after a rocky start," smiled Inspector Hartley. "I expect you'll all be joining the force in a few years. We could do with such talented investigators on the team!"

I felt myself glowing like a microwave full of pride.

We were all laughing and talking when suddenly there was a great bang.

"WHERE IS SHE?" boomed a familiar voice.

"I'm sorry, sir, you don't have clearance. . ." I heard the policeman stationed outside the room squeak.

"No, Boris, put him down . . . PUT HIM DOWN," I heard Doris shout.

Inspector Hartley flung the door open just as Boris had lifted the unfortunate policeman over his head as if he were a fluffy pillow.

"What is going on here?" demanded Inspector Hartley, but he had to jump out of the way as a stampede of circus performers thundered into the room and flung themselves at me.

"Oh, Tomato, Tomato. . ." wept Fanella, tears running into the fake moustache she was wearing. "I think you are dead as doo-doo."

"It's 'dead as a dodo', dear," corrected Doris, giving my shoulders a squeeze.

With another bang, Luigi came tumbling in, towing Buttercup on a lead behind him. The inspector gasped and grabbed Miss Baxter's arm, pulling her behind him at the sight of the lion. The poor police officer, only just recovering from being tossed around by Boris, turned completely white, gulped and fainted dead away.

"WHERE IS THE SCOUNDREL? THE VILLAIN?" yelled Luigi fiercely. "IF YOU HAVE TOUCHED ONE HAIR ON POPPY'S HEAD, PREPARE TO BE VICIOUSLY MAULED!" Unfortunately Luigi's heroic appearance was rather ruined when Buttercup gave a big yawn and flopped comfortably on the carpet, turning on to her back so that Ingrid could rub her belly. Marmalade the cat slunk in and curled up next to Buttercup, rubbing his face on the lion's side and purring loudly.

"It's OK, Luigi, I'm fine. They arrested Gertrude."

I peeked around the shoulders of a still-weeping Fanella, who was getting my shirt very soggy.

"Oh, good-oh," said Luigi, dropping down on the floor next to Buttercup and stretching out his long legs. "Not sure I'd have really been able to go through with the mauling, Pops. Terribly messy business, you know, makes a chap quite queasy." He tickled Buttercup behind the ear. "And I'm not completely sure my little angel was really clear on the plan here. Look at that face! She's just a kitten!"

Inspector Hartley looked as if he was about to strongly disagree, but then, realizing he still had his arm around Miss Baxter's waist, he turned the colour of a sunburnt beetroot and started stuttering his apologies instead.

"Well, it's been quite an evening," said Miss Baxter, smiling around at all of us. "One that I think even Dougie Valentine himself would have found a bit stressful!" We all laughed. "So I suggest dinner and a nice cup of hot chocolate around the campfire while we all calm down."

This suggestion was met with cheers, and everyone headed back to the campfire outside the big top tent. As we sat there, curious students and teachers who had heard the kerfuffle of police sirens drifted down to investigate. Soon there was a full-blown party taking place. Everyone was laughing and telling jokes and stories, singing and toasting marshmallows, and Miss Baxter made a speech about how me, Kip and Ingrid had recovered the stolen ruby and caught the criminal and everyone cheered. Nobody wanted the night to end, so when Miss Baxter said there was no curfew that night and lessons would resume tomorrow afternoon, everyone cheered even louder. Looking around me, I realized that this was exactly what I had hoped school was going to be like.

Without really knowing how it happened, or who suggested it, we all found ourselves squeezed into the big top for a real show. I smushed in with the others, enjoying being part of the crowd for once, just as excited as everyone else, even though I had seen the performances countless times before. I oohed and ahhed when the fearless Luigi managed to tame a ferocious-looking Buttercup – even though I regularly rubbed that lion's belly and knew she was really a big softy. I laughed until my sides hurt as BoBo and Chuckles performed their slapstick routine, falling all over each other and juggling plates of wiggling jelly. I held my breath as The Magnificent Marvin sawed Doris in half and then put her back together the wrong way round before making her disappear completely in a puff of smoke, only for her to reappear on top of the high wire, where she performed a fantastic tightrope-walking routine. I clapped and clapped until my hands were sore as Tina and Tawna flipped and somersaulted on the backs of their beautiful white ponies. I peeked through my fingers as a blindfolded Sharp-Eye Sheila threw knives at a spinning target to which Luigi was tied – each knife missing him by a whisker. I stared wide-eyed as a snakey-hipped Fanella danced with flaming batons and swallowed massive fireballs. I shouted in disbelief when Boris Von Jurgen lifted a small car over his head. I gasped when Pym leapt from trapeze to trapeze, tumbling and spinning almost out of control. And in the end, when they all took their bows, I joined the crowd and cheered until I had no voice left in me.

The applause went on for ever. Looking at Ingrid and Kip's faces in the glow from the stage lamps, I saw that they had been completely transported by the magic of the circus, just as I had seen happen to so many kids before. This time it was different, though, I thought with a warm glow spreading through me like a bowl of strawberry custard. This time the audience wasn't made of strangers. They were my friends. I slipped my arms around Kip's and Ingrid's shoulders, grinning widely. "So," I laughed, "What's next?"

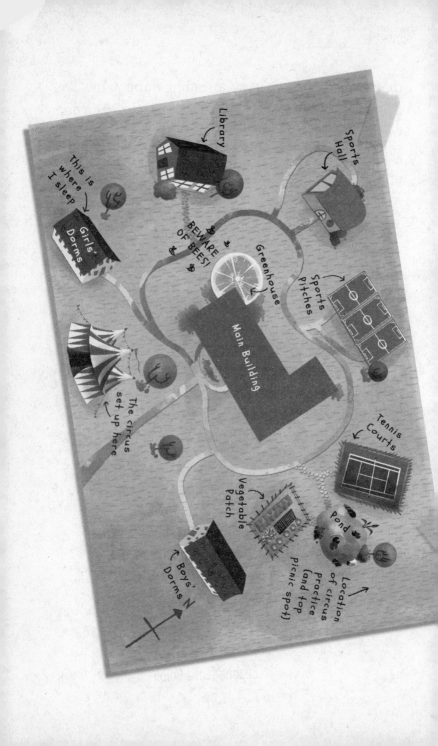

ACKNOWLEDGEMENTS

As with my Oscar acceptance speech (witty, gracious, self-deprecating) I have frequently written and rewritten the acknowledgements for my first book in my head over the years. Now that the moment is here I am overwhelmed with gratitude and by how lucky I am to be surrounded by wonderful, supportive people, but equally aware that these thank-yous need to be shorter than the rest of the book. While there is no band to play me out and tell me that my time is up, I will try my best to keep this brief.

This book really wouldn't exist without the Montegrappa Scholastic Prize for New Children's Writing. My thanks to Giuseppe and the team at Montegrappa for their dedication to the written word, and for the beautiful dream of a pen with which I will be writing the rest of Poppy's adventures. It is thanks to your passion that I am able to write these words. Big thanks also to everyone at the London Book Fair and The Independent, as well as the brilliant and beautiful Cerrie Burnell, for all your kindness and support. I am also grateful to my fellow shortlistees, Rohan, Nicola S, Nicola T and Kate – talented, funny, generous people. This is the start of big things for us! A big thank you (and a huge picture of Kenneth Branagh) to my agent, and Anne Shirley-esque kindred spirit, Louise, who was my champion from the very beginning. To the whole team at Scholastic, I can't say enough about how great you are and how excited I am to work with you, thank you for helping to turn my idea into this beautiful book that I can hold in my hands – you really did make my dream come true. Special thanks go to my wonderful editor Lena who was clever and kind and patient and who transformed this book into something better than I could ever have imagined.

Boundless thanks to my mum, dad and my brilliant brother Harry. I love you all so much and I'm so lucky to be related to three of my favourite people in the whole world. Thank you for always believing that this would happen. To Nan and Paps for all the adventures, for feeding my greedy imagination and for peddling this book to every single person they know. Love and thanks to the rest of the Bailey/Wilson clan and especially to my fairy godmothers AJ and Lissy. Also, to my second family, the Grigsby/Wellers. Thank you for welcoming me into your family and for all your love and support in all things over the last seven years. Also, thank you for inviting me on a nice holiday and still being friends with me after I had to stay at home and write this book – I guess it was all worth it in the end! I have to say a special thank you to Imogen Weller, my beautiful niece and my inspiration. She is all the best bits of this book rolled into one. To Mary, my very first reader, and to Chris, I love you both and please know that there will always be room for you in my castle. To Becky and to Daisy, lovely, lovely friends I am lucky to have. To my dear friend Lynda, with champagne cocktails to follow.

To Kristen and her gorgeous family, who will single-handedly get this book into every home in America. I love y'all!

Finally, to Paul. You made this possible in every way. I love you and I like you. Best friends.

Kip and Ingrid didn't seem to see the funny side of my mummy impression.